W9-AZQ-718

FIC
HER
Herman Labyrinth

DATE DUE			
APR 6			
MAY 12			

Accelerated Reader

51779
Labyrinth

John Herman
ATOS B.L: 4.5
ATOS Points: 6   UG

SARATOGA SCHOOL LIBRARY
MORRIS, IL

LABYRINTH

▣ ▣ ▣

John Herman

PHILOMEL BOOKS ▣ NEW YORK

B+T
7/01
10.43

PATRICIA LEE GAUCH, EDITOR
Text copyright © 2001 by John Herman

All rights reserved. This book, or parts thereof, may not be reproduced in
any form without permission in writing from the publisher,
Philomel Books,
a division of Penguin Putnam Books for Young Readers,
345 Hudson Street, New York, NY 10014.
Philomel Books, Reg. U.S. Pat. & Tm. Off.
Published simultaneously in Canada.
Printed in the United States of America.
Designed by Semadar Megged.
Text set in 11.25-point ITC Cheltenham.
Library of Congress Cataloging-in-Publication Data
Herman, John, 1944–
Labyrinth / John Herman.
p. cm.
Summary: As he struggles to cope with his father's suicide and his mother's
possible remarriage, fourteen-year-old Gregory is plagued by recurring
dreams that make him question what is real.
[1. Dreams—Fiction. 2. Fathers and sons—Fiction. 3. Suicide—Fiction.
4. Family problems—Fiction.] I. Title.
PZ7.H43153 Lab 2001
[Fic]—dc21
00-041685
ISBN 0-399-23571-X
1 3 5 7 9 10 8 6 4 2
First Impression

For G.B.H.

A BOY'S WILL IS THE WIND'S WILL,
AND THE THOUGHTS OF YOUTH ARE LONG,
LONG THOUGHTS.

◙ ◙ ◙

At that time the Athenians were much troubled by reason of the tribute they had to pay to Minos, the king of the Cretians. Each decade Athens was forced to convey its ten most promising youths to Crete, there to be eaten by the Minotaur, a monster half bull half human that dwelt in a twisting labyrinth from which no one had ever been known to escape. Here the Minotaur lived, feeding on its victims.

BOOK ONE

□ □ □

"Don't worry," his father said. "You'll never have to go."

They were sitting at the breakfast table with the cold winter light streaming through the window. In the sky the pale moon floated like a distant world.

"How do you know?" Gregor asked. He was dressed in his gray school uniform, striped, with the logo of the Pioneers on the pocket. "How do you know I'll never have to go?"

"Because," his father said matter-of-factly, "I'll fix it."

His father was number two in his division of the Bureaucracy, so it was true he could fix things—sometimes. Once Gregor had believed whatever his father told him: that he didn't have to worry; that he could fix things; that everything would be all right. But that had been once upon a time—when he was a kid.

His mother sat looking at the table. She was a pretty woman who had been worn down by the years so that there were wrinkles now at the corners of her eyes.

"Anyway," his father said. "Who says it would be so terrible if you went?"

"No!" his mother exclaimed fiercely. "I won't have it!"

Why is Mom always upset? he thought. Why is she upset because I might be chosen one of the Ten?

"Now, now," his father said, frowning. "Don't get excited, Mother. I was just speaking hypothetically, to make a point. It's time the boy grew up."

"I won't have him going," she said.

"Well, don't worry, I'll fix everything. Isn't that right, Gregor?" And he winked.

Gregor didn't wink back.

1

Awake!

Gregory sat up in bed. He had been dreaming—dreaming of winter though it was May and he had kicked the bedcovers off.

Ten little Indians, he thought. Ten little Indian boys!

Something was happening to him. He was being overwhelmed by dreams. It was as if some other world was colliding with his in his sleep. And yet when he woke he could hardly remember what the dream had been. He would catch the tail end of it disappearing round the corner like a man running out of sight. But it would leave him shaken for days, disoriented, frightened.

He lay panting, waiting for the dream to subside. The curtains blew inward, billowed like sails. Like some ship far out at sea with no one on board but himself. Himself and, in the farther room, perhaps still awake, his mom.

He rested his back against the headboard. The clock glowed at him like a weird eye from across the room: 11:23 P.M.

Shouldn't there be a moment when life made sense? Some moment when you understood? Or was this all there was? Lost like this, floating between dream and waking . . . ?

Ten little Indian boys!

Sometimes when he woke with his eyes still shut, he imagined he was still in the old house where he had grown up. Before they had moved. Before his father had died. He could picture the radiator, the crack in the wall like the profile of a convict, the bookshelf with the books his mom and dad had given him; could hear the sound of water from the brook at the bottom of the hill. It was all so real that he couldn't remember where he actually was. Then he would open his eyes, would look around—and reality would come flooding back.

"It wasn't his fault," his mom had said. "You have to understand, Gregory—he wasn't well."

He tried not to blame his father. He tried.

Because he was dead. Gone forever.

Gregory swung his legs out of bed. He slipped on his jeans, sneakers, T-shirt. In a moment he had stepped through the open window into the night.

The wind ruffled his hair. The stars twinkled overhead like distant worlds, dazzling and incomprehensible. He groped to the edge of the roof, careful not to make a noise, and, swinging into the maple, dropped safely to the ground.

Gregory paused in the shadows of the house where he would still be hidden if his mother had heard, but everything was quiet. Insects whirred in the grass. The wind moaned. Somewhere in the distance a dog howled.

He emerged onto Highridge Drive, the moon shaking

overhead. When he had gone out at night with his father, his dad had always carried a flashlight against the oncoming cars. For years he had thought his dad the greatest guy on earth. What had gone wrong?

Leaving the road, Gregory descended toward the lake. He skirted the field where the earth had been plowed up in great ugly mounds as if against some unlikely invasion. At the bottom of the hill where Union cut Lakeshore, he crossed the four lanes without incident.

Mr. Power lived in the large white house overlooking the lake.

"He wants his own guy as number two," his dad had explained. "It makes perfect sense. He doesn't want the previous CEO's heir apparent."

He was trying to be fair, his dad. That was just like him: fair—and dead.

Gregory checked that no one was watching. Then he leapt the low brick wall that surrounded the house. He emerged on top of the small rise where Mrs. Power had planted her rock garden. From here he could spy into the patio and the study below.

He hunched down, feeling his scalp prickle in the darkness. He still felt haunted by his dream. He had come to the house before, any number of times. Because he wanted to prove that his plan could be carried out. That it wasn't just words. Empty words.

He could hear the words his father had used. The highsounding gospel of good deeds and fine intentions his father had preached, which had broken up against the rock of reality like some boy's ship constructed of toothpicks and string.

"It's not what you say, son, that matters, and not what you believe about any deity, but how you behave, and how you treat your fellow man, that is the one and only measure of your worth in this life. . . ."

Maybe he would kill Mr. Power after all. Just half a push and he would do it. You could bet on it. Because Power had killed his father as sure as if he had shot him through the chest. Had cheated him out of his job. Played with him. Made his life miserable. Then fired him.

Gregory settled against the rock. He could smell the earth, the odor of grass, the lake where it was gooed with algae from the fertilizer from people's lawns. He closed his eyes.

Gregor pushed his chair back from the breakfast table.

"I'd better be going to school," he said.

"That's right," his father agreed. "You don't want to be late."

But his mom stopped him before he could leave the room.

"Don't leave without kissing me," she said.

He bent and kissed her, and he felt the old love, older than anything else in his life, well up like a sickness. But he pulled away.

He paused at the front door before leaving for school, and he could hear his parents in the kitchen still arguing.

Why is Mom so upset because I might be chosen one of the Ten? he asked himself again. *She had changed— ever since his motorcycle accident the previous year. It was as if she was always expecting something awful to happen. But what?*

He tried to recall his dream of that night but couldn't. And he gave an involuntary shudder. Outside the snow stretched as far as he could see. The trees were sticks against the white. He opened the door, and the cold slapped him in the face like the flat side of a sword.

Gregory woke with a start. He had been dreaming again, right here in Mr. Power's garden!

He could fall asleep wherever he was: in a car, in class, over his homework. The dreams, so far as he could see, weren't like regular dreams, they were too consistent and continuing, like real life only weirder, as if he was in contact with some other world. Yet at night he couldn't sleep at all, he would lie awake tossing.

He recalled his dad moving about downstairs that last year after losing his job, unable to sleep.

"I don't want you making the same mistakes. Like a curse. A curse you just have to live with."

"Dad!"

"Though maybe it would be better to end it. Make room for someone else. But I don't want you making the same mistakes."

(It wasn't his fault, his mother had said. You can't blame him. It was a sickness. A mental illness.)

Because his dad had shot himself in a motel room. Had blown off the top of his head. . . .

Mr. Power had appeared in the study downstairs. Gregory could see him moving about preparing to go to bed. Setting a book on a table. Turning off a light. He hated that fat pasty middle-aged used-up wuss. Hated that he was alive and his dad was dead.

Gregory braced himself against the side of the rock. He could see the top of Power's head. He could take him out with a head shot. Or downward through the shoulder into the heart. He decided for the bald spot on the top of the skull. Now Power had paused, his back turned. Gregory sighted with care. He eased the imaginary trigger.

POW!

2

"You should off him," Jed said.

They were smoking cigarettes by the boulder in the field above the high school, though this was against the rules and they could be suspended for it.

"Off him?"

"Sure. Didn't the son of a bitch kill your dad?"

It made Gregory sick when Jed said this. Because he thought Jed was right.

"How would you do it?"

Jed shrugged. He was two years older than Gregory, with ruddy skin and dark, handsome features.

"There're lots of ways to off a guy. You own a gun?"

Gregory shook his head. He could smell the warmth of the wind across the new May grass.

"Well, you could get one."

It was true, he had seen guns when he broke into houses that winter while playing hooky from school.

"I once knew a guy ran a man over," Jed observed casually. "Ran him over in a Chevrolet. That's as good a way as any."

Gregory listened to this with amazement. It was remarkable how many ways there were to kill a man.

"He didn't get caught?"

"Nope. You do it at night."

"How do you get the guy to come out?"

"You could call him. Make an appointment. That's just a for instance."

Gregory could imagine calling Power, telling him he had to see him. He'd even tell him who he was. "This is Albert Levi's son," he'd say. "It's confidential." That would get him to come for sure.

Gregory tried to imagine Power's face as the car careened toward him. How scared he'd look. He'd see Gregory at the wheel, and he'd know it was for real. "This is for what you did to my dad," Gregory would shout just before the car smashed into him.

Gregory remembered the time their car had run

over a dog. He had felt the tires go over the body, bump bump. Had felt it in his own stomach.

And he knew he could never kill Mr. Power with a car.

"I think I'll shoot him," he said.

"Whatever." Jed shrugged. "I'm just telling you about the car as an idea. It's your call."

Gregory had met Jed during detention one afternoon when the late afternoon sun was streaming against the classroom wall. The teacher was supposed to stay at the head of the room, only everyone knew he was a goof-off; so when he put them on the honor system and waltzed off for a smoke, Jed ambled to the front of the room, sat in the teacher's chair, put his feet on the desk, and announced, "Class dismissed."

Gregory had been sitting at the back of the room staring out the window. Dreaming about how it used to be before his family moved. Before he cut classes. Before his dad was dead. Now he started to watch Jed from under his brows.

Gregory knew who Jed was, of course. Everybody knew who Jed was. The kind who once upon a time Gregory would have had nothing to do with. Always acting up. Always getting into trouble.

Actually, Jed looked pretty cool, with his James Dean good looks and his upper lip that jutted out so he could dangle cigarettes. But mostly what Gregory admired was the way he didn't take crap. All the crap that went down. The crap they had to eat daily.

The girls started to laugh—the older girls and even the goody-goodies like Alicia. But mostly Virginia, who sat across the room (Gregory knew exactly where she sat) and who had straightened up and was watching Jed with large glowing eyes.

"So who's going to split?" Jed had asked. "No takers? All a bunch of losers?"

Jed gave his characteristic shrug.

"Okay," he said. "Have it your way." He ambled toward the door. "Toodleoo, suckers. *Sayonara!*"

That's when Gregory stood up.

That's how he got to know Jed.

3

Gregory broke into other people's houses. It had started that winter when he played hooky from school. Because he hated this new school. Hated this new town. Hated this new life without his dad.

Hillcrest was on the South Side, in a residential area. If you walked west along Pinkney, pretty soon you came to spacious lawns with large houses that were empty much of the day because everyone was out working, like his mom. Gregory would circle to the back and find an open window or a back door, and then he'd have a place to hang out for a few hours and stay out of the cold.

He knew that his mom would have a fit if she found out what he was doing, but he didn't care. He never stole anything, unless you counted milk and juice and an occasional cookie or piece of cake. He'd settle down to read or watch television or just float from room to room, poking around. It was kind of a magic time, inside those houses, as if he was in a different space from the rest of the world. A different universe.

Sometimes, floating from room to room, he'd have the weird feeling that this had all happened to him before. One afternoon, for example, while reading a magazine in somebody else's house, while looking at a picture of a freighter tossing and heaving through the waves, he had been seized by the conviction that he had been on that ship; had somewhere experienced exactly that combination of winter sunlight, loneliness, and a boat far out at sea.

As a kid these sensations used to overtake him all the time. He had called them cross-over moments (he couldn't say why, the name had just seemed right). They could overtake him anyplace, in the middle of whatever he was doing, weird and uncanny, as if precisely this thing had happened to him before. The experience would last only an instant, but during that time it was as if he had broken through to another realm, more intense than the everyday, yet scary and inscrutable, as if his everyday reality was only a dream.

There were also cross-over places, the most important of which was in the basement of his old house, where a huge slab of granite stuck up like the spiny back of a monster. The stone, his father had explained, had been too hard to blast out when the house was being built, so they had constructed the house around it. And there it remained, below them like a dragon in a cave. He was careful about playing down there because he knew it was a dangerous place, dark and foreboding, as if it opened into the center of the earth. You might cross over down there and never get out.

As he grew older these cross-over moments had become less frequent until finally they stopped altogether. And then that winter, when he broke into houses, they had started again.

4

"Have you ever had the feeling that things have happened to you before?" Gregory and Jed were again sitting outside school smoking cigarettes.

"What are you talking about?" Jed asked.

"Oh, I dunno." Gregory hesitated, not certain whether to continue. He had never talked to anyone about this before. "Let's say I'm looking at that tree and suddenly I have this feeling that exactly this has happened to me before. I mean that I've been sitting here talking with you and looking at that tree. The sensation will last just a second or so, but during that time I feel certain that this has all happened."

"That happens to everybody," Jed said casually.

"Does it?"

"Yeah, it's called déjà vu. It's French. It means you've seen it before."

Gregory sat thinking about that. He was always surprised by the strange things that Jed knew.

"How can you have seen it if it's never happened before?"

"I dunno. It's never happened to me, actually. I just heard about it."

"It used to happen to me all the time," Gregory admitted. "When I was a kid. It would overtake me anytime—just for a minute. But for that second it was like this magic. I had forgotten all about it—but now it's started again."

"Oh, yeah?" Jed didn't sound all that interested.

"I was looking at this picture in a magazine. Actually, I had broken into this house and I was all alone. The sun was shining through the window, and I sat on the davenport and opened a magazine and saw this picture of some old freighter, it must have been from South America or something. But suddenly I had this feeling—it was like this *conviction* actually—that I had seen exactly that freighter somewhere before."

"So? Maybe you did. In another magazine."

"No, it was as if I had been *on* that freighter. Had known it intimately—y'know what I'm saying? But I never have."

Jed shrugged.

"I wouldn't worry about it if I were you."

"I'm not *worrying*. It's just—strange. It made me feel . . . weird, as if I were living two lives or something."

Crows had perched in a tree across from the boys and seemed to be watching them from across the field. Gregory could hear the wind in the grass.

"I saw this thing on television," Jed said after a while. "About other universes."

"What do you mean?"

"There's this theory that there are an infinite number of universes. Parallel universes. We're just one out of an infinite number. So maybe we're living our lives in other universes at the same time."

"That's crazy," Gregory said. Jed's words made him feel spooky.

"Well, that's what the man said on television. At least best as I could make out. Hey, it was you who started talking about this stuff, Greg-o. I'm just telling you what I heard."

"I wouldn't believe everything I heard on television," Gregory said.

"Hey, Greg-o, don't get all snotty. This happens to be science—you can look it up for yourself. Besides, I learn more from television than I ever do at school."

5

He seemed to be in a kind of labyrinth, with passages leading in all directions, lit by a glimmering light as from dirty ice reflected from the walls. He proceeded downward with growing anguish in his heart, as if rushing toward a destination. Occasionally he emerged into larger spaces, caverns glimmering with frost, with the drippings of stalactites that hung from the rocky roof like the fangs of beasts. Immense birds roosted in the crags, their wings fanning the air. Bones were piled in corners, the skulls and skeletons of the creatures the birds had fed upon.

6

Gregory went to the school library to look up about parallel universes. Maybe that would help him understand about his dreams. About his crossing over into some different world.

He took out a book called *Cosmological Conundrums*, but he couldn't understand what it was saying. It had to do with quantum mechanics, which seemed to hold that you could never know all there was to know about the inside of an atom. He didn't need quantum mechanics to tell him that. The way he figured it, you could never know all there was to know about the inside of *anything*.

At any rate, some scientists had proposed that there were an infinite number of universes, and that the division of atomic particles was the gateway into these other worlds.

All this struck Gregory as pretty far-out. He didn't see how any of this helped him with his sense of crossing over. Could it be that he was breaking through to another universe? In his dreams? In the cross-over moments? Did any of that make any sense?

He leafed through the book, reading about the big bang, about black holes. It all seemed like science fiction to him. Looking up, he noticed Virginia sitting a few tables away. He could only make out her back, her shoulders slightly rounded, the sweater soft-looking where it followed the line of her body; but just looking at her like that from across the room, he felt himself shiver.

7

"You mean Mr. Power's *daughter*?" Gregory said in dismay.

"Yup," Jed said. "The very one."

"But that's—*fantastic*!"

"Why is it so fantastic?" Jed said with a shrug. "How

many Powers do you think there are in this dink town? Don't sweat it, Greg-boy. She's cool. She hates her old man."

Gregory was dumbfounded. Virginia Power was Mr. Power's daughter! The daughter of the guy who had killed his dad!

Did anything make any sense?

Gregory had first noticed Virginia during a basketball game in the new gym with the kids stamping and hooting in the grandstands and the ball resounding off the wooden floor. Somebody had pointed her out because she was one of the hot girls at Hillcrest. In fact she didn't appeal to him at first. She was sort of exotic looking, not American blue-jeans cute, but sort of Egyptian or something, with dark hair and large dark eyes, which she highlighted with eyeliner (Gregory observed this later, when he got to know her). Actually, she looked cool like that, but it took a little getting used to, at least for Gregory (his mom never wore makeup).

She was kind of highwaisted (maybe because her legs were so long), and her clothes were a little snazzier than the other girls', with these cottony, short-sleeve sweaters, black or red, that clung to her so it was hard to take your eyes away. In fact the more Gregory looked at her, the better looking she became, until pretty soon she was the only girl he wanted to look at.

There were different reports about her. Many thought she was stuck-up. She smoked in the girls' bathroom. She cut gym and assembly. She showed up a notable number of times at detention. She was reputed to be a troublemaker.

But others said that she was real cool. Nice when you got to know her. Not snobby. And everybody agreed that she was in love with Jed Turner.

8

Gregory decided to break into Mr. Power's house. He went at midday, when it was less likely that anyone would be there. He didn't admit to himself why he was going, but he knew anyway. He wanted to get closer to Virginia.

The air was warm with spring, water was running in runnels along the side of the road. It was great to be out of school. If he had his druthers he'd never go back.

When he got to Power's he vaulted the wall as he did at night, then circled to the back. His biggest fear was dogs. When he reached the patio he jimmied the French door.

He breathed the perfumey air of the living room. The couch was as brightly colored as a dress. The place was decorated in chinon and silk, with French-like lamps that Gregory imagined might break if you looked at them too hard. There was a picture on the side table of Virginia and her mom, both dressed in expensive white outfits.

The study was something else, done up in a Mexican motif, with Mexican rugs on the floor. This was Power's hangout. There were pictures of bullrings and bullfights on the walls. And, mounted above the door, the head of a great, horned bull.

Virginia's room was on the second floor. Gregory mounted the stairs cautiously. The room was surprisingly tidy, decorated in white and yellow with tasseled curtains and bedspread. A Keith Haring picture on the wall. A poster of the Stones. A postcard of James Dean. Very girl.

He hesitated in the doorway. He could see out the window to where the lake shimmered on the horizon. Maybe he should leave. Then he moved stealthily to the desk. He picked up her diary. He didn't intend to read it, but he opened it anyway.

". . . called last night and spoke until three. Told me about his motorcycle, some trip last winter—I don't know what. It wasn't important. Just his voice. God, why do I love him?! It's like this sickness. Is that what we mean by love? I told him I had to hang up, but he said if I did he'd never speak to me again. So I had to wait for ten minutes while Daddy was outside, with just this silence between us. I was so scared—scared he wouldn't talk to me again . . ."

Gregory turned to another page.

". . . because I love him. And he's so cruel. Just uses me. Plays with me. Doesn't give a damn. I know that, and yet I can't tear myself away. Like some dream.

Some nightmare. So I don't believe there's any such thing as love. Just this. This torturing."

Gregory closed the diary.

He knew he should get out of there. Something drew him to Virginia's bed nonetheless. There was a special odor, sort of powdery, the way Virginia must smell. He lay down. He closed his eyes.

"So who do you think is going to get chosen?" Muffet said to Till.

It was winter, and the Pioneers were standing outside the dining hall in the blue light of evening, a dust of snow covering the paving stones. Gregor had gone out to get some fresh air. His knee ached him from the motorcycle accident.

"I dunno," Till said, his Adam's apple going up and down as he spoke.

"Lemon's for sure," Babcock said. He leaned forward, the tallest of the circle, hunching his shoulders against the cold.

"You think so?"

"Sure."

"What about you?" Muffet said to Babcock.

"Me?" Babcock flushed with pleasure. "You think so?"

"Of course Babcock will be chosen," Till said. "Babcock and Lemon are for certain."

"What about him?" Boob said, pointing at Gregor. Gregor was taken aback. He had been standing at the edge of the group smoking, the cigarette cupped in his hand.

"Me?" he said, and he felt himself color.

"Sure," Boob said. "Why not? Doesn't Mr. Brown love you?"

Brown was their literature professor.

The others looked at Gregor coldly, sizing him up.

"It's possible," Till said after a pause.

"We're all possible," Muffet said. "We're all Pioneers."

"Sure," Babcock said. "What about Boob?"

And they laughed.

But their skepticism annoyed Gregor. Not that he wanted to be one of the Ten. But why should someone like Babcock be considered a shoo-in and himself a dark horse? It was only because he was a loner.

"Personally," Muffet said, studying his toes, "I'd just as soon not be chosen."

"Oh, yeah? Why's that?"

"Oh, I dunno," Muffet said, still not raising his eyes. "It's just a feeling. Nothing I can put in words. I'll just leave the honor to someone else."

"What I don't understand," Boob said, "is why there are never any girls."

"Yeah. What about feminism? What about equal opportunity?"

"They couldn't cut it," Babcock said. They all looked at him.

"Whattaya mean? What's to cut?"

"The mustard," Babcock said. "Just take it from me, a girl couldn't cut the mustard."

Gregory awoke and had no idea where he was. For a moment he lay listening to the stillness. He felt a hollow sickness in the pit of his stomach. The dream! It was pursuing him wherever he went. He was and he wasn't that other boy. He was and he wasn't in that other world. And yet, while he dreamt it, it seemed more real than anything in his own life.

Then he remembered: Virginia's room! It came flooding back to him. Anyone could have found him here! The thought made him sick. It was unthinkable that Virginia should ever know that he had broken into her house.

He swung off the bed and set about hurriedly fixing the room, making sure it was in order. He paused at the door; everything seemed in place. Finally he slunk away down the stairs, out the back door, over the wall.

9

Gregory didn't want any more trouble with his mom. He had enough already. Which he would never have thought possible. Because of the way he felt about her. The love. But such was the fact.

And now she had a boyfriend. A boyfriend! The very word made Gregory puke. Richard was his name, and he was a professor at the university, where his mother worked.

"I know what a tough time you're going through," Richard said, and his tone made Gregory sick. Richard sat on the edge of the couch as if he was afraid he might break something. Gregory was the something he was afraid he might break.

"Do you, Richard? That's big of you."

Richard gave a sigh. "I know you're suffering," the sigh said. When he thought he could get away with it, he'd offer Gregory little pep talks, pearls of wisdom culled from his own vast experience of life.

"Each of us has some monster to face," he'd say with a frown. "Yours is pretty bad right now, Gregory— I don't deny it. But you've got to tough it out—that's part of growing up."

Richard dressed in plaid shirts and corduroy sports jackets with elbow patches. Real academic. Only Gregory happened to know that his clothes came from Brooks Brothers and cost about a million bucks. So what he really looked like, in Gregory's opinion, was a wonk.

When Gregory asked him what he did, Richard told him that he taught the sociology of ideas. Gregory didn't know what that meant. His own father had been Senior Vice President at TechnoMagic.

Richard had written a book called *Archetypes and History,* a copy of which he had given to Gregory.

"I don't know how much of this will make sense to a guy your age," he had said. "But I want you to have a copy, anyway."

Gregory could have done without that crack about his age.

Richard inscribed the book: "To my friend Gregory."

Gregory didn't consider Richard his friend.

Gregory had tried to read the book, but it was pretty heavy going.

Now, as they sat in the living room, while his mom checked on dinner and Richard sucked on his drink, Richard said, "Archetypes are like the stories you're studying in Greek mythology." Richard liked to give little lectures, as if he was in front of his class. To give him his due, he knew a lot of stuff. The only problem was, Gregory didn't want to hear his lectures.

"Like Perseus and Andromeda," Richard pursued. "Or Theseus and the Minotaur. Have you read about how the ten most gifted youths of Athens were sent every decade to be eaten by the Minotaur?"

"Sure sucks for those gifted youths," Gregory said.

"Soup's on," his mom called. "Come on, you guys. You can continue the conversation at the table."

"So Theseus volunteered to go kill the Minotaur," Richard continued as they made their way to the dining room. But Gregory had heard quite enough from Richard about the heroes of yore and the monsters we all have to face. Richard was something of a monster himself, so far as Gregory was concerned.

"Archetypes," Richard said when they were sitting at dinner (it seemed to Gregory that Richard was sharing their dinner more and more frequently), "are the stories people use to build their sense of reality. The stories they keep telling themselves. Like dreams."

"Like dreams?" Finally Richard had said something interesting.

"Yes. The great psychologist C. G. Jung believed that our dreams are made of archetypes."

Gregory thought about that for a bit. He tried to ignore the fact that a piece of salad had stuck to Richard's front tooth.

"You mean that we dream these archetypes?"

"Yes—much of the time."

"So it's sort of as if the archetypes were dreaming us."

Richard looked at him and blinked.

"I'm not sure I'm following you on that, Gregory."

"Well, the archetypes come first, right? I mean we're not making them up, if I understand what you're saying. So—are we dreaming the archetypes or are the archetypes dreaming us?"

"That's very interesting," Richard said, and he laid his fork down by the side of his plate.

"These archetypes are sort of 'there' before we dream them, right?"

Now it was Richard's turn to think.

"Well, I suppose so. In a manner of speaking. In the sense that they exist, if that's the right word, before any particular dream. Any particular person."

"What do you mean?" his mother, who had been listening, now asked. She sat at the head of the table with her two men to either side.

"Well, there's yourself," Gregory said, "and there are these archetypes that Richard is so keen to tell us about—and they were here first. So maybe the archetypes are what's real, and it's we who are the dream."

Richard gave a brief laugh.

"I suppose you could think of it that way, though I never have. I'm afraid I haven't made myself very clear. This is harder than I thought."

For a moment Gregory considered asking Richard about his own dreams. About parallel universes. But he thought better of it. Richard knew a lot of stuff, but in the end he was just a wonk. And he didn't want him more intimate with their family than he was already.

After dinner Richard invited him to join them in a game of Scrabble, but Gregory declined. Instead he excused himself and went to his room. If he had Jed's motorcycle he'd be out of there. Zoom! Out of there with never a look behind.

10

"Pioneers!" Principal Alexander peered out at the auditorium from under his shaggy brows, his keen eyes glittering. Under the light his polished head gleamed like a patch of frozen snow.

"Pioneers! Ask not what your country can do for you. Ask what you can do for your country!"

Gregor sat in the second row toward the left, where he had a good view. Everyone had thought the announcement would come in January, but the month had passed without word, and after a while Gregor put the Ten out of his mind. Then in the third week in February the Pioneers had been called into the assembly hall in the middle of the day, and, despite himself, Gregor felt his stomach tighten.

"As you know," Principal Alexander continued, "every ten years certain Pioneers are selected to represent this great nation in the Mother Country—one of the highest honors our country can bestow. It is an honor not just for those ten young men, it is an honor for all of us, for it is on the shoulders of the Pioneers that this responsibility lies. Be proud to bear it! Be proud to uphold the welfare of the Homecountry!"

Thunderous applause. Gregor applauded too, though not as hard as the others.

"In every life," Alexander continued, "there comes a moment when we are tested. Through that trial we are proved. By means of that testing we pass from innocence to wisdom, from childhood to adulthood. When we were children we thought as children, but now we must put aside childish things."

Again an outpouring of applause. Alexander paused, peering out from under his shaggy brows, his eyes glittering. He had a deep voice, which he played like an organ, and his eyes, which were gray, could be as hard as steel, but had never been known to be soft.

"Pioneers," Alexander called. "It is time to select the Ten!"

Gregor hunkered down in his chair. Recently he had been troubled by dreams, probably because of all the suspense. Now at least it would be over.

"You all know JT Hammer," Principal Alexander continued. "The captain of the Pioneer Patriots—one of the most outstanding Pioneers I have ever known. JT, please come to the podium."

JT bounded onto the dais. He was a tall young man, with ruddy skin and dark, handsome features, slender for a football star; but anyone who had ever seen him play would never forget his speed and elusiveness on the field. Now he stood next to Principal Alexander accepting the applause of the school.

"Pioneers," Alexander called, quieting the audience with his outstretched hand. "Pioneers, although, as a Senior, JT is not in the proper Form to be selected as one of the Golden Ten, he has nonetheless volunteered to assume a place in their ranks. I know you will want to support JT."

Everyone sprang to his feet, clapping and hurrahing. JT stood at the front of the stage modestly acknowledging their cheers.

Alexander now waved a sheaf of envelopes over his head.

"In these envelopes," he called, "are the names of

the other nine young men who have been granted the privilege of representing this nation in MC. Before I open them, let us bow our heads in prayer."

There was a rustling as everyone shifted, lowering his head. Gregor peered out from the corner of his eye, and he saw Babcock three seats away, his head lowered, his ears glowing a ruby color in the heated auditorium.

Gregor's name was the seventh called.

II

Gregory sat up with a jerk. What was that voice in his head, those forms, that story? In his confusion he thought for a moment he was still in his dream. He couldn't distinguish anything, only the beating of his heart.

Then he heard someone downstairs. It was after midnight. He imagined it was his father. Only after an instant did he remember that that was impossible. Who was it then?

He slipped out of bed and reached for his baseball bat.

He stopped in the dark at the top of the stairs, listening. He could feel the slight pulse of the house, like a man breathing. Someone was in the kitchen—it didn't sound like his mom.

What if it *was* his dad?

He went down the stairs quietly, clutching the bat. He flipped on the kitchen light.

It was Richard.

"Gregory!" Richard looked alarmed.

For a moment the two stared at each other. Gregory noted that Richard wasn't wearing his sports jacket and that his shoes were off.

"Get out!" Gregory said.

"Wait a minute, Gregory."

"Just get out."

"Gregory, your mother and I . . ."

Gregory took a step forward. He wasn't sure what he was going to do with the baseball bat, and that was scary.

"Gregory!"

Gregory's mother was standing in the doorway in her nightgown.

"Put the bat down," his mother said sternly.

Gregory half turned and looked at his mother. Then he let the bat rest against his shoulder.

"Gregory," she said, "I asked Richard to stay."

Her voice was firm—not angry but not very inviting.

"Stay for what?"

"Gregory," Richard said, "I know this is hard for . . ."

"Just shut up!" Gregory said.

"Gregory!" his mother snapped.

Then for a while all three of them were silent.

"Listen, Gregory," his mother said. "You want us to treat you like an adult, don't you?"

He looked at her but didn't say anything. He felt his eyes sting.

"Why don't you put down the bat," his mother said.

Gregory looked at Richard. Then he laid the bat down on the counter.

"Adults need each other," Richard said, "just the way kids do. Especially when things are tough."

"We don't need *you,*" Gregory said.

"That's not for you to say," his mother said, and her voice was cold again.

"This is Dad's house," Gregory said.

"This is *my* house," his mother said. "I'll decide what happens here."

"Let me talk to him," Richard said.

Gregory picked up his bat from the counter.

"I'll decide who I talk to," he said. And he left the kitchen.

Upstairs he lay on his bed staring at the ceiling. And again he weighed in his mind whether anything had any meaning or whether everything was a pointless joke. A dream. Finally he crawled under his covers. Ten little Indian boys, he thought. Ten f-ing little Indian boys!

12

"How did you do it?" Alicia kept squealing. "Just tell me, how did you do it?"

"I didn't do anything," Gregor said. "It just happened."

He couldn't help feeling pleased. He'd always liked Alicia, but she'd never paid him much attention before.

Babcock, who had also been selected one of the Ten, was surrounded, as usual, by admirers.

"It's up to us now, buddy," he called across to Gregor— a most unusual occurrence. And he offered an earnest, maturelike expression. Gregor, smiling back, tried to look earnest too.

Gregor walked home by himself. Why had he been chosen? Was it a good thing or bad? Everyone seemed to think good. A great honor, as Alexander said. Blah blah blah. So why was his mom so opposed? He'd be away for a long time, of course. Doing what? He didn't even know. Nobody had said.

He hadn't expected to be chosen. Why him? He wasn't out of the ordinary. Just himself. Or if he was a little out of the ordinary, it wasn't in a way to get selected for MC. Quite the opposite, he would have thought.

Take their uniforms, for example. Everyone wore these red ties and gray striped jackets, so you knew at a glance they were Pioneers and went to the elite high school. Well, that was all right, he supposed—though sort of stupid. Why, after all, should everyone wear the same uniform? Everyone wasn't the same, were they? So he had taken to loosening his tie. Not a big deal, just a little loose, so he could breathe. Only it drove the teachers crazy. They would stop him in the hall. Would send him to detention. Would threaten to kick him out of school.

Or the length of your hair. Your hair wasn't supposed to touch your collar in the back. Well, okay. But there again—what was the big deal? It just so happened that Gregor liked his hair long. So he let it grow. And then, before he knew it, he was in trouble. Once he had even been stopped by Principal Alexander, who told him that if he didn't cut his hair by the next morning, he wouldn't be allowed back in school.

The Ten were supposed to be the best and the brightest to represent the Homecountry in MC. The best athletes. The best math students. The true Pioneers, rah rah! Not skinny guys who wore their hair too long and loosened their ties. So why had he been chosen?

And was it a good or a bad thing to be chosen? And if good (as everyone, including Principal Alexander, seemed to think), then why was his mom against it? And what if anything could his dad do? And why had JT decided to go? He'd be damned if he could say.

None of it made much sense.

13

"Narcolepsy," Jed said.

"Narcolepsy?" Gregory had never heard the word before.

"Sure." Jed was working on his motorcycle, crouching on his drive while Gregory watched. "It's like this sleeping disease," he said. "Like epilepsy or something—only sleep."

Gregory stood above Jed thinking. Narcolepsy! Is that what he had? He could ask Richard—he'd know that kind of stuff. But he'd be damned if he'd ask Richard.

"It's like just suddenly I'll fall asleep," he explained. "For no reason."

"Yup," Jed said. He was fixing the carburetor, a rag dangling from his back pocket. "That's it precisely."

"When I wake up," Gregory continued, "I feel awful! As if I can't sort out what's real and what isn't."

Jed hadn't stopped working on the motorcycle. He had bought the bike secondhand for three hundred dollars and had fixed it up himself. It could reach ninety miles an hour, easy.

Gregory loved to ride on that bike. He could feel each gear as it kicked into place. Each bump of the road. Sometimes he'd keep his eyes to the side, with the trees flipping by like a pack of cards.

He'd made the mistake of telling his mother.

"I won't have it," his mom had said. "Do you hear? It's out of the question! Motorcycles are dangerous, Gregory. Do you want to knock out your brains?"

"I'm not going to knock out my brains."

"That's not what the statistics say."

"I'm not a statistic."

"Gregory—this isn't open for discussion. I'm telling you no!"

"I don't think you have the right to do that, Mom. I didn't ask to move to this town. To leave my friends. My school. If I'm going to live here, I've got to fit in."

"Gregory," he could see the muscles working in her jaw, "I didn't want to move here either, but this is where we are, and this is where we're going to stay. I won't be emotionally blackmailed. And I won't have you killing yourself on a motorcycle. *Hasn't there been enough death in this family?*"

That was the conversation about the motorcycle. But he rode it anyway.

"Narcolepsy," Jed now said, standing up and cleaning his hands on the rag. "It can be fatal, like sleeping sickness or something—you never wake up."

"How do you know all this?" Gregory asked.

"I saw on TV about this guy who was in a coma for over a year. When he woke up he wrote down all his adventures. It was like he had traveled to other lands."

It made Gregory feel creepy.

Jed walked around to the front of the bike and checked the air pressure with his hand.

Jed lived with his mother in a small house in the blue-collar section of town, not far from the meatpacking factory. Sometimes, when the wind was blowing wrong, the air would taste of the rancid meat.

Jed's mom did clerical work during the day. Jed's father had disappeared years ago, no one knew where. Jed didn't like to talk about him.

"Sure, my old man," he would say with a sneer. "He split years ago. Not that I blame him," he'd add, "living with my mom and everything."

"So what's with you and Virginia?" Gregory asked to change the subject from the creepy topic of his dreams.

"Whattaya mean?"

"I mean, are you a couple or what?"

"A couple?" It seemed to irritate Jed. "Is that what she says?"

"I don't even know her, Jed. I'm just asking."

"No, we're not a *couple.* We just sort of hang out together. You ever had a girlfriend?"

"Sure," Gregory said. "I mean I had this girl at my other school who liked me okay . . ."

"Then you know how it is," Jed interrupted. "You like a girl, you hang out with her, you fool around a little. The next thing you know, you're a *couple.*"

Gregory didn't answer. If Virginia liked *him,* he wouldn't shrug it off like that.

"Why doesn't she like her dad?" he asked after a bit.

"How should I know? The guy's an SOB. Isn't he the guy you want to off?"

The two boys were silent while Jed continued with his bike. After a time he straightened up and wiped his hands.

"You know what I'm thinking?" he said. He sighted out over the roofs of the low-lying houses across the street. "I'm thinking of getting outa here. For good. Getting away from school. From everything. Y'know?"

"Yeah," Gregory said dourly, thinking of Richard and his mother. "How you gonna do that?"

"On this chariot of fire," Jed said, patting the bike.

"Where you gonna go?"

"To New Orleans, probably. Someplace we can't be found. I've got a scheme."

Gregory looked at his friend with interest.

"Oh, yeah? What's your scheme?"

"I'm not at liberty to tell you right now. Let's just say it's something I've cooked up with a friend. You wanna come?"

"I can't come," Gregory said bleakly. "I don't have any money. Besides," he added, "there's my mom."

14

Often, when his father had come home early from work (which had happened more and more frequently that last year), Gregory would find the light on in the garage. His dad would be in old clothes tinkering with some piece of machinery. He earned his living in an office behind a desk dressed in a white shirt and tie, but what he really loved was to work with his hands. He would have made a great mechanic. Or a carpenter. Or even a plumber. For he understood all things mechanical, all machinery, all electricity, and there was nothing he couldn't fix.

When Gregory saw the light on in the garage, he would go out to be with his dad. Those were some of the best times they had together. He loved watching his father's hands, strong and compact, adept at whatever they did, adjusting the carburetor or changing the spark plugs, the parts laid out neatly on the side table, the light clamped into the open hood.

"I ever tell you about the time I fell off the tractor?" his father would ask. Gregory had in fact heard the story numerous times, but he was always glad to hear it again.

"We had a place in the country," his father would begin, "and I was friendly with the farmer down the road. Well, one day he asked me whether I wanted to drive his tractor. I was thirteen or fourteen, about your age, and had never driven a tractor before, but of course I couldn't resist. So I jumped up onto the seat and off I went."

"How did you know how to drive it?" Gregory asked.

"Oh, I could drive anything with wheels," his father said, and, so far as Gregory could discover, that was true.

"Well, I was driving along," his father continued, "when my parents drove by. And my mom, your grandmother that is, stuck her head out the window and gave such a holler that I looked around, and just then the tractor went over a bump and I went tumbling off the seat and broke my arm." And his father chuckled.

"You know the lesson there?" he concluded. "Never drive a tractor with your head on backward."

The two laughed over that.

His dad took a rag from his back pocket and wiped his hands.

"Tell me about the time you drove to Chicago," Gregory said.

"Oh, that was later, when I was about nineteen. I'd promised this fellow I would drive his car to Chicago for five hundred dollars, a lot of money back then. Well, the night before I was supposed to go, I cut my hand on a rusty piece of metal. So I had to drive by myself nine hundred miles with my bandaged hand held over my head like this because of the throbbing."

"Cool," Gregory said. He wanted to drive off like that and never look back.

"Why didn't you just keep on going?" he asked, caught up in the excitement of thinking about it. His father looked at him and sort of winked.

"Where to?"

"Oh, I don't know. Anyplace."

"You mean like California or something?"

"Sure—anyplace."

"What do you think I'd have found when I got there?" his father asked.

"I dunno."

"When I got there," his father said, "my feet would still have been on the very same earth. Do you know what I'm saying, Gregory?"

But this wasn't what Gregory wanted to hear.

"Maybe not the *very* same," he said.

His father studied him for a moment in silence.

"Well, maybe not the very same," he said. "But close enough. Besides," he added, "I had your grandmother to look out for." And he put his hand on Gregory's head and gave it a rub.

15

Gregor's mother wept when she heard the news. She turned absolutely green. It annoyed him, actually. After all, it wasn't everyone who was chosen.

"They'll ship him off across the ocean to God knows where. We'll never see him again."

"Mother, Mother! Now watch what you say." His father became agitated if anyone breathed a word against MC. "Of course we'll see him again. Just think of the honor!"

"The honor? To be sent to the end of the earth to serve a bunch of barbarians?"

It ended with his mother retiring to her room. What was wrong with her, anyway? What was wrong with being chosen one of the Ten?

"There's nothing wrong," his father assured him. "It's a great honor."

"Then why is Mom so upset?"

"Oh, you know your mother. She has her own ideas. On some subjects, however, one should keep one's opinions to oneself."

"Well, if being chosen for the Golden Ten is such a disgrace," Gregor said, "I wonder why there are plaques and monuments in their honor all over the country."

"Precisely!" his father concurred. He took a turn around the room, smoothing his hair back with both hands. He had dark hair and a small dark mustache, and Gregor had always, secretly, been proud of the way his father looked; but he had noticed recently, with sadness and something of a shock, that his father's hair was going thin in the back.

"Still," his father added more thoughtfully, "given your mother's attitude, perhaps it's just as well if you don't go. I'll see what I can fix up at the office."

"Whatever!" Gregor said in disgust.

He had never heard of anyone being dismissed from the Golden Ten—but neither had he ever heard of anyone trying. He couldn't make heads or tails of it. He washed his hands of the whole affair.

16

Jed kept pacing back and forth across the floor of the garage. Gregory had never seen him so worked up before. "I'm out of here," Jed snapped. "I'm outa this dink hole!"

The other afternoon Jed had drunk a flask of rye whisky, then driven his motorcycle into the country, where he rode through a farmer's field in a large figure eight, jumping hillocks and pushing the motor to well over eighty miles an hour.

Gregory tried to show enthusiasm while Jed related his adventure.

"I wished you was there, Greg-o," he'd explained. "I'd of let you take a spin all by your lonesome. I knew I should get out of there, but what the hell, the harm was done, I might as well enjoy the benefits."

Gregory tried to imagine Jed whipping through that field on his bike, the mud flying up while his wheels dug a deeper and deeper trench behind him.

"There was this jump right in the middle," Jed continued, "where you could work up a pretty good head of steam. I took it ten or twelve times. I was thinking I ought to split when I looked up, and who do you think I see bouncing along on his tractor but old Farmer Hick, his face all red-like and his shotgun in the air."

"Shotgun?"

"Yeah—a shotgun. I mean, what is this, the Wild West or something?"

"Jesus, Jed—you might have gotten shot."

"Don't worry," Jed spat. "I'm not going to get shot."

Gregory could see Jed's jaw working in and out as he glowered under his brow.

"What did your mom say?"

"My mom?" Jed looked up as if the question surprised him. "What do I care what my mom says?"

Then they were silent again.

"So what are they going to do?" Gregory asked after a while.

Jed threw the rag from his back pocket onto the ground.

"They've suspended my license," he said with disgust. "But this cop told me they'll probably take the bike away."

"The bike!" Gregory's heart sank.

"Don't worry," Jed said. "They're never going to take my bike."

"How can you be so sure?"

"Because I won't let them."

Gregory didn't say anything for a while.

"What about—you know—chariots of fire?"

"That's on more than ever," Jed said. "I'm telling you—I'm outa here."

Jed looked at him hard. It was spooky when Jed looked at you like that. Gregory wasn't sure he even knew whom he was looking at.

"There's no way they're taking this bike, Greg-o! What you don't seem to understand is that the entire adult world is just a bunch of pussies."

17

"No way, Mom," Gregory said. "No fucking way."

"Gregory! Watch your language."

Gregory couldn't believe her. It was just like an adult to worry about your language at a time like this.

They were in the kitchen, by the counter that divided the room from the dining area—the last place where he had seen his father alive. It had been winter, his father hadn't looked well. Pasty. Unhappy. But acting cheery. Putting on a false front. As if he could take care of everything. And now his mother was saying that she wanted Richard to move in.

"Richard's not moving in, Mom."

She sighed heavily.

"I wish I could make you understand."

"Understand what? Richard? You want me to understand *Richard*?"

"Me," she said. "I want you to understand me."

Outside he could see the buds on the trees. It was the second spring. The second spring since his father had died. Stupid! It was all so stupid.

"What do you want me to understand?"

"That I'm a *person*. That I'm lonely."

There were tears in her eyes. He couldn't stand it when she did that. When she cried. It was so unfair. But he wasn't going to give in.

"I know you're a person, Mom. I know it. And I know you hurt. But that's no reason . . . that doesn't mean . . ."

He stopped, not wanting to put it in words. He could if he had to but he didn't want to. Didn't want the words to stand between them forever.

"Gregory—it's just on a trial basis."

"No trial! No!"

"Gregory, I've known Richard for years. It's not as if he was just someone who came along."

"That makes it better? You think that makes it *better*?"

He couldn't stand that she had known Richard before, when his dad was alive. Did that mean she had liked him before his dad had died?

He didn't understand adults. They seemed to him *unclean*.

"Gregory—you know I love you, don't you?"

"Yes, Mom."

"And you know I loved your father."

But that he wouldn't answer. Standing there not looking at her, above the counter where his father had kept the Jim Beam. Mixing himself a drink. Talking to them about the day, telling them something amusing while his mom stood at the sink preparing dinner. Back then, when they had been happy.

"Answer me, Gregory. You know I loved your father."

But he wasn't going to give it to her.

"Ooh!" she said, and her voice was angry. "That's so *unfair*. How can you question that I loved your dad? How? That hurts me so much, Gregory. I can't tell you how much that hurts me."

He felt a shiver of panic when she said that. That he had hurt her. Because of course . . . because . . . But he wasn't going to give in!

"Maybe you loved him once, Mom. But look at what you said. You *loved* him."

"Gregory, Gregory! Do you think I don't love him now? Do you think that?" She was almost pleading with him. "But he's gone, Gregory. Don't you understand? He's dead!"

When she said that he thought he was going to die. He turned away, and for a while they were both turned, weeping. But in truth she wasn't much of a weeper. Less than he. And she had collected herself before him.

"Gregory," she said. She had sat now on the stool, and she touched him on the shoulder with one hand. "I'm sorry you're so unhappy. I'm unhappy too. But I have to go on with my life. If I break down, we both break down. I carry us both. Maybe you don't under-stand that . . ."

"You don't carry me, Mom."

"Excuse me, Gregory, but I do. Maybe you don't see that now, but you will someday. I can't be justifying myself to you endlessly. You'll have to take some of this on faith."

He waited sullenly, not wanting to argue, not wanting to say more that would hurt her. But he opposed her now completely. He rebelled at the idea that she carried him.

"Richard lives on the other side of town," she persisted. "It's unfair to make him go back every night. It's pointless. I see that this is tough for you, Gregory. But you've got to help me. You've got to give me this. You've got to trust me."

"He's not moving into Dad's house," Gregory said.

18

Immense birds roosted in the crags, their wings fanning the air. Bones were piled in corners, the skulls and skeletons of the creatures the birds had fed upon. He had to keep running, as if he had lost his balance. He heard a shrieking bellowing reverberation. Finally he emerged into a level place, a cavern lit with flickering uncertain light. The cave smelled rotten, bloody, moldy, dank, foul. The birds uttered strange cawing sounds, which echoed from the rocks like laughter.

19

"What's the news about the motorcycle?"

The two boys were standing between classes in a patch of sunlight at the end of a corridor. Gregory had balanced his books on the radiator while Jed remained chewing a pencil.

"I told you," Jed said. "They're not going to take my bike."

"Oh, yeah?" Gregory said. "You still thinking of splitting?"

"More than ever."

"Well," Gregory said, thinking grimly of Richard and his mother, "I want in."

Jed's eyebrows went up.

"Chariots of fire?"

"That's right," Gregory said. "Chariots of fire."

Jed lifted a leg and balanced it against the radiator. He cradled his chin in his palm, studying Gregory.

"We're talking some pretty heavy stuff here," he said.

"That's okay with me."

"You think you're up to it?"

"Just tell me about the scheme," Gregory said morosely.

Jed looked out the window. He didn't answer for a moment.

"Well," he said after a while, "I guess it depends on the stars."

"The stars?" Gregory could never tell when Jed was kidding him.

"Sure."

"You mean you believe in that?"

"Sure," Jed said. "I think this world's gonna end soon."

Gregory was taken aback.

"Whattaya mean?"

"You know—like the Book of Revelation. The conjunction of the planets."

"That's crazy."

"You think so?" Jed looked at him thoughtfully. "What about you and your dreams?"

That shut Gregory up. He didn't know what to say.

Jed continued to stare out the window. "If you want in," he said, "you can't try to sneak out once you know what's up."

Gregory made a face.

"I won't try to sneak out."

"Okay," Jed said. He shrugged. "Then we'll have to talk to Virginia."

20

"So Gregory wants to join us," Jed explained.

Jed, Gregory, and Virginia were sitting in Jed's garage, a bunkerlike structure of poured concrete cluttered with parts from old motors, radios, tools, empty cans of motor oil, piles of newspapers, broken chairs leaning against the walls, and the seat of a dilapidated Chevy with brownish scars from cigarette butts.

"You want to come along?" Virginia said, looking at Gregory from under her brow.

She was sitting in a rickety chair with her hands dangling from the broken armrests. She had delicate wrists and long tapering fingers, and she let her hands hang as if she had forgotten about them and then would suddenly snap them up like lively little animals. She swiveled now to look at Gregory.

He wouldn't have picked Virginia as Jed's type. She always dressed nicely and smelled of perfume or powder or something (he recalled the odor from her room), and her laughter was sort of throaty, and when she looked at you she wouldn't try to hide what she was doing but would gaze straight at you for as long as she pleased.

But it was clear she was crazy about Jed. You could see it in her eyes whenever she looked at him. She loved to ride on Jed's bike, and she looked great like that, with her arms around him and her knees pointing up. Maybe she wasn't Jed's type, but Gregory could sure see why Jed liked her.

She was two years older than Gregory, which was like forever.

"I just want to know the scheme," Gregory said, and blushed as he said it.

"I see," Virginia said. "How old are you, anyway?"

"Fifteen."

"He is not," Jed scoffed. "Don't lie to Virginia."

"Well, I'm fourteen. What difference does it make?"

"Fourteen?" Virginia said, and she raised her eyebrows and looked at Jed significantly.

She had dark brown eyes, almost black, with long lashes and heavy eyebrows that almost met, and her skin was white and smooth, and her nose was aquiline and set at a slight angle to her face, and this was the only flaw in her person, if you considered it a flaw, which Gregory didn't.

"Why are you interested?" she pursued.

"I want to get away." He hesitated for a second. "From my mom. From the whole scene."

"You mean at your place?"

"Yeah," he said, "at my place."

She nodded as if that made perfect sense.

"Well," she said, "it's all right with me."

So that was settled. Gregory felt a spurt of excitement.

"What exactly is the scheme, anyway?" he asked.

They both looked at him. "You tell him," Jed said casually. He was leaning against the wall cleaning his nails with his pocketknife.

"There are these tunnels under the town," Virginia said. "They lead everywhere." They were called the Tombs, she explained—this labyrinth of tunnels for the electrical and sewage systems that ran in all directions.

"I've done a little poking around down there," Jed said. "Believe me, it's no picnic. You could get lost forever. But with a flashlight you can make out okay."

"Cool," Gregory said.

"Yeah," Jed continued. "Of course you've gotta know what you're doing. It's cramped and hot and dark. If something happened to your flashlight you'd be screwed."

"I read about this guy," Gregory said, "who was trapped in tunnels like those, so he laid down this string so he could find his way out. He was a prince or something."

"Theseus," Virginia said. "But it was his girlfriend who laid down the string. And it was a spider's web."

"Whatever," Jed said. "I don't need any string. The point is, there's an entrance in the boiler room in school that leads across town to the Emerald Building. You come out right behind old man Power's office."

"The building's all locked up at night," Virginia said. "But the tunnels lead under the building—right under the locks. We could get into my father's office. But here's the problem. There's a wall in the tunnel about fifty yards before the building. There's this little crawl space at the top—but it's too small for Jed and too high for me."

"That's where you come in," Jed said.

"You mean maybe I could fit through?" Gregory said.

"Yeah, that's the idea. You up for it?"

"Sure," Gregory said. "I'll get through."

It excited Gregory—the idea of the tunnels, of breaking into Mr. Power's office, of getting even. He knew he was getting deeper and deeper into something that his parents wouldn't like, but he didn't care.

"So what are we going to do when we get there?" he asked.

Jed looked at him steadily.

"*We* don't do anything," he said with a kind of drawl. "*You* do. You're gonna steal some jack. Power keeps money in his office—he puts it there every Monday. Virginia knows where."

"He takes a wad to his office every week," she said, and her eyes looked excited and sort of challenging.

"You'll have to do the actual heist," Jed said. "I'll be waiting in the tunnel. We'll need to wait until next Monday, but we're sure to clear a couple of grand. And then we're outa here."

"New Orleans," Virginia said. "Here we come!"

Gregory felt like doing a little jig but he restrained himself; he didn't want Virginia getting exercised again about his age.

"I've gotta say," she added after a moment, "this

wasn't the coolest time, Jed, to go raising hell on your motorcycle."

Jed didn't bother to answer.

"Remember those houses you broke into?" he asked Gregory, scowling. "Well, I want you to break in and steal a gun."

"What do we need a gun for?" Virginia asked.

"Just shut up," Jed said. "I'm not talking to you."

"Okay," Gregory said after a moment, though he didn't like the idea of a gun. "I'll steal a gun."

So that's that, Gregory thought. I'll break into a house. I'll steal a gun. I'll run away. His mom didn't need him anymore, anyway. Now she wouldn't have to *carry* him any longer.

Jed had turned to Virginia. "Let's get one thing straight," he said. "I'm in charge here."

"Who said you weren't?"

"I don't like your rich-girl attitude. I don't want any of your rich-girl lip."

"What do you mean?" Virginia flushed.

"Like that crack about my motorcycle."

"Jesus, Jed—I didn't mean anything."

"Just don't give me any of your snotty, rich-girl atti-tude, that's all."

21

Gregory caught up to Virginia on the sidewalk and walked beside her trying to think of something to say. He could see she was still angry from the exchange with Jed.

"Jed can be a pain in the ass," he said after a bit.

"He's such a bastard," she burst out, tossing her head. "What makes him think he can treat me like that?"

The wind lifted the edge of her hair so he could see her small ears, curled like little shells. He remembered how he used to go poking in the tide pools, searching for periwinkles and polished pebbles. He couldn't think of anything else to say, and they walked in silence.

"Have you ever been in love?" she asked suddenly.

He could see her out of the corner of his eye, her face still flushed and angry.

"Yes," he said after a moment. "Yes, I guess I have."

"Well, what *is* it?"

They were silent, thinking; and he was thinking of what he felt for her.

"I guess," he said, "it's like what they said in biology class, about missing salt from your body. About how you'll crave it."

They continued walking in silence while she bit her lip.

"So," she said after a while, "if we weren't missing something, we wouldn't love—is that what you mean?"

"I guess so. But I think you can be pretty sure we're all missing something."

"So we love because we are *inadequate*."

"I can believe that," he said. "That agrees with what little I know about love."

She continued beside him without speaking, apparently thinking about what he had said. They were under the trees now, where the new leaves cast small shadows onto the ground.

"It's tough about your dad," she said after a time. "He worked for my dad, didn't he?"

"Yeah," Gregory said bitterly. "He worked for your dad."

"My dad's a shit," Virginia said matter-of-factly.

He felt gratitude for her having said that. It bound them together, somehow. Her hating her dad. His confusion about his dad. Their being here together.

And he wanted to tell her something about himself.

"I have these dreams," he said, though he had never told anyone about the dreams except Jed.

"Dreams?" She wrinkled her brow. "What kind of dreams?"

"I dunno. Weird. I think maybe I'm in touch with another world."

She stopped and looked at him hard. The wind was in her hair, lifting it, and he thought, why does she have to love Jed?

"What are you talking about, Gregory?"

He smiled. "Don't worry, I'm not crazy."

"I don't think there are any other worlds," she said carefully. "I don't think that's possible. What makes you think something like that, anyway?"

"Jed told me this stuff," he said, "about how there might be parallel universes."

She considered him before answering.

"I wouldn't believe everything Jed said."

"I've been reading about this myself," he said. "About science. Black holes, for example. Time stops in black holes."

"That's science fiction."

"No," he laughed. "It's true. So why not parallel universes? There are probably millions of them. We're probably walking around in a parallel universe right now."

"How can I be walking around in a parallel universe?"

"Why not? Maybe you're in a parallel universe when you dream. And what about when you're dead? Or before you're born. I think there are infinite universes. You're not just trapped in this stupid one forever."

22

"We haven't a thing to worry about," Gregor's father exclaimed. "Believe me, it's all under control." And he gave his wife a hearty look—the kind Gregor had grown to mistrust.

"The Boss is back," he started, "and we had a little tête-à-tête."

He rubbed his hands together, smiling at his wife and son. He had returned from the office that Friday and had sat everybody down at the table.

Gregor wasn't certain what he felt. What if his dad had actually gotten him dismissed from the Golden Ten? Was that good? What would he say at school? That his mom had cried, so his dad had pulled strings and gotten him off?

"The Boss is a very busy man, you know," his father continued. "Nonetheless, when he called me into his office today, he was beaming, as if my inventory report had especially pleased him.

" 'So,' he said as I sat down, 'I hear there's cause for congratulations.'

" 'It was just my duty,' I told him. 'I had a difficult time accounting for all the pencils, but . . .'

" 'Pencils?' the Boss said, looking perplexed. 'No, no, no! We're not here to talk about pencils. I mean the selection of your son for the Golden Ten!'

" 'Ah,' I said. 'The Golden Ten! Yes, I suppose it's quite an honor.'

" 'Suppose!' he cried. 'Come, come! We all know what an honor it is to be appointed to the Golden Ten!'

" 'Yes,' I said. 'Yes, of course.'

" 'The welfare of the nation depends on the Ten,' he said.

"There was a moment of silence while we looked at each other. Suddenly he leaned forward, almost like a father, and spoke in a lowered voice.

" 'Is there anything I can do for you?' he asked. 'Just between the two of us?'

"This was the opening I had been looking for.

" 'Well, you know, Your Excellency (sometimes on special occasions I call him Your Excellency), I did want to have a word with you. And in fact it did have to do with my son and this question of his selection.'

" 'Yes, yes. What's on your mind?'

" 'It's his mother, Your Excellency. I believe I've spoken to you about her before.'

" 'Yes, indeed, I remember. And how is her health?'

" 'About the same. Maybe even a little improved— until the question of this selection arose.'

" 'I see.'

"Now he frowned more in the old manner and sat back at a greater distance in his chair.

" 'Well, what is it, then?'

" 'Well, to get to the point, the thought of our son being sent away . . .'

" 'Stop! Stop!' And he held up his hand as if there was something he didn't want to hear.

" 'My dear fellow,' he said after a moment, 'listen to me. You have to understand first of all (and he held up one finger) that in my official capacity I cannot allow myself to hear any complaint against one of the fundamental institutions of this nation. I am sure you understand my position. Second (and here another finger), I want to repeat that being chosen for the Golden Ten is one of the highest distinctions this country can confer. You are to be congratulated—and that is something which your wife must be made to understand. Finally (yet another finger), you should know that any family whose son has been selected in this fashion will be taken care of for the rest of their lives. Do you think we do not know how to reward our heroes? Rest assured, dear fellow, that Gregor's being selected is just the beginning of a series of rewards that shall gladden the remainder of your days. Your son must certainly remain one of the Ten.' "

His father had stopped, his face frozen in a broad smile.

"That's your good news?" his wife said after a moment.

"Yes, indeed. I believe I have reproduced the Boss's words with accuracy. I always listen to the Boss with special attention."

"Well, if that's all your boss had to say," Gregor's mother said, "then he's a horse's ass—and you can tell him that for me."

"But, Mother . . ." and the smile died on his face. "What after all did you expect?"

"Expect?" she said. "Expect? I didn't expect you to be such a fool."

23

The Ten met each day at the Institute for Advanced Political Studies to prepare for MC. They wore special blue uniforms with gold caps, which the other guys loved, though Gregor thought them a little stupid. But he kept this opinion to himself. Except for a lame messenger boy, the Ten were the only high school kids there.

The other guys were excited to have been chosen for the Ten. But whether because of his mother or not, Gregor was less thrilled. He was flattered, sure. He enjoyed the attention of the other kids—especially the girls. But something about the whole business felt fishy.

The boys were taking a brush-up course on the language of MC, of course. (All Pioneers learned MCish from the time they were seven.) The MCers spoke a broad, nasal tongue, with shortened vowels and harsh pronunciation. They didn't like the Homecountry language (they thought it snooty and made fun of it—not without a touch of envy).

"The MCers aren't fond of *fancy* words," Professor Enk, a tall distinguished man who had actually spent time in MC, told them.

"You mean we've got to speak like *them*?" Furst blurted out.

Professor Enk wrinkled his brow and looked even more serious than usual.

"Mr. Furst, must I remind you how much we owe to our distinguished friends in MC?"

Then he paused, and for a moment he remained staring at the floor.

"Let me give you boys a piece of advice," he continued. "When in MC, there's no point in drawing more attention to yourselves than necessary. I'd keep as low a profile as possible."

"I didn't know MC invented *baseball*," Babcock said after one of the classes. The boys were standing under the clock by the main hall watching the older students from the Institute stream past. Gregor, as usual, was standing to one side.

"Well, I think they invented it—in a manner of speaking," Boyer said. "I mean they invented it, I suppose. But then they didn't really *play* it, y'know?"

"I don't think you should say that when you get to MC," Gregor said.

"Whatchya mean?" Boob asked.

"Well, I think the safest thing is just to say that they invented *everything.* Like glass and candy and spit."

"Jesus," Boyer said. "What a cynic."

The MCers were powerful drinkers, and it was considered a breach of decorum to fall behind, so the boys were taking a course in drinking. Gregor became adept at pouring his liquor on the ground or spilling it into a plant—whatever was necessary to escape the endless succession of toasts.

There was also a course on religion. The official cult was built around the State. The MCers' ancient religion was similar to that of the ancient Greeks on Minos, who had sacrificed to bulls. Most of the "born again" believers, however, were located in the backcountry of MC, where the boys wouldn't venture.

The last class was Survival Skills, where they practiced jujitsu and boxing. Gregor was delighted to learn these sports, but he was puzzled about their purpose.

"Why do you think we have to know this stuff?" he asked Lewis one afternoon while they were in the locker changing back into their uniforms.

"I don't know," Lewis said. He was a sandy-haired boy, about Gregor's size, and less full of himself than some of the other kids. "This whole thing is a little bizarre."

"You think so?" Gregor asked. He was relieved to hear that someone else shared his impression.

Lewis looked at him, and for a moment he seemed on the point of saying something, but then apparently he changed his mind.

The instructor for Survival Skills was a short, trim man with a brown mustache and bristling eyebrows— a real gung-ho type. He paced back and forth at the front of the room with his pointer clutched behind his back, speaking in a crisp, measured tone.

"Counter insurgency!" Major Green would bark. "Green Berets!" Back and forth he'd pace, talking in a clear, determined voice while the boys tried to understand what it all meant.

Slowly, however, Major Green's voice became less crisp. He paced back and forth with less determination. His brow furrowed. He looked at the boys and shook his head.

During the third week he suddenly stopped talking altogether. He entered the room, sat at his desk, and remained silent. After ten minutes he got up, gave a sigh, began pacing—but still said nothing. Suddenly, "This doesn't make any sense," he said. "You know, we're not going to do this anymore. Today we're going to watch movies."

And thereafter, Survival class was spent watching old Fred Astaire musicals.

24

Gregory slipped out of his house at night, crossed the road, and headed for Mr. Power's. He was going to spy again, but this time it wasn't on Power. This time it was on Power's daughter, Virginia.

He waited by the wall where the looming shapes of the houses were cut by the patches of light from the windows. No one had seen him. He could still turn back. . . . Then he vaulted the low wall and, crouching, moved forward through the dark.

The wind was up, tossing the branches of the trees. He felt his heart beating. Now he could peer into the study. Probably he would see no one. He should turn around and leave. But he circled the house, still keeping close to the ground—and suddenly the light was shining onto the patio through the Venetian doors and he could see Virginia at the dining room table, her father at the head of the table and her mother (it had to be her mother) pacing back and forth across the room, gesticulating violently.

Crouched in the darkness, his heart beating, Gregory watched. Virginia and her father sat at the table, he a tall gangly man with large hands and long ears who leaned forward as if he was about to fall; she with her head lowered as if to shield herself from some blow; while the mother continued back and forth, her mouth working, silent on the other side of the glass.

Gregory kept his eyes fixed on Virginia, her cheeks flushed, her gaze lowered; and, watching her, he experienced a sudden rush of sympathy so intense that, for the moment, it was as if it was he sitting in that room, trapped and vulnerable, and not the girl.

He turned and slunk away into the night. He hated Power—hated that pasty wuss who had destroyed his dad. But Power didn't really matter anymore. And he knew he wouldn't be coming back.

25

Gregory heard the thud from the other room. He rushed into the kitchen and saw his mother lying on the floor, the oven door open, the rack protruding. He ran to her and saw the raw red burn slashed across her forearm.

His heart thumping, he lifted her and carried her out of the kitchen. She was moaning, her eyes fluttering. "Put me down, Gregory," she mumbled, but he continued into the living room (he was afraid he might drop her), where he laid her gently on the sofa.

He had never seen his mom pass out before and he was terrified.

"So stupid," she moaned. "On the stove rack."

"I'll call 911."

"No—I'll be all right."

She was deathly pale, and he wondered, in his panic, whether you could die of a heart attack from a burn like that.

He dialed 911, feeling the fear in his throat. Everything could turn upside down in a second.

He rode with his mom to the emergency room, where Dr. Kozinsky bandaged her arm in loose gauze while he scolded her for her carelessness.

"Kitchens can be very dangerous, very dangerous. More accidents happen in kitchens than in any other room in the house."

"I thought it was bathrooms," his mother managed to say.

"Ah!" (turning to Gregory) "You see, she's getting better. Already she knows more than I."

Dr. Kozinsky sent her home with a painkiller; Gregory was to apply a salve every three hours and change the dressing.

"Now you're the man of the house," Dr. Kozinsky said solemnly, and placed a hand on Gregory's shoulder. "I want you to take care of your mother."

"I'm sorry," his mom said during the taxi ride home. "It was so stupid of me."

"Don't talk like that, Mom. It wasn't your fault."

He helped her out of the car, and he could feel her lean against him.

"I have to go to bed, Gregory. I'm done in."

"Of course, Mom." This was how things should be.

"Please," she said, "call Richard for me."

"What for, Mom? Why do we need Richard?"

"Gregory—please. He'll want to know. I want him to know. Besides, he'll have to go to the store for supplies. You can't drive."

26

"That sucks about your mom," Virginia said. She touched his arm, and the touch seemed to radiate across his body, as when a pebble falls in a pond. "Will she be all right?"

"I guess. It's a third-degree burn."

"Is there anything I can do?"

"Naw, that's all right."

"You know," she said after a moment. "I've been thinking about our scheme. Maybe we should put it off for a while."

Gregory had been thinking that himself, ever since his mom's accident. He didn't see how he could leave her, Richard or no Richard. On the other hand, he didn't see how he could back out on Jed.

"What would Jed say?"

"I don't know. Do you want me to talk to him?"

"No," he said. "That's okay. I can take care of myself." He didn't want her talking to Jed on his behalf.

Standing close to her, he wanted to reach out and touch her, though he knew he couldn't.

"How is it with you and Jed, anyway?"

"Oh, I dunno." She shrugged again. "You can see."

It didn't seem fair to him. Nothing seemed fair.

"What about you and your dreams?" she asked.

"The *parallel universe.*" He looked to see if she was mocking him but she didn't seem to be.

"Worse than ever."

"No kidding!"

"Yeah. But now I want it to continue."

"Whattaya mean?"

"I want to get to the bottom of it. No matter what."

"Well," she said after a moment, but not without sympathy, "it's too far-out for me. I don't really know what you're talking about."

"Neither do I," he admitted. "I'm just trying to make sense of what's happening to me. It's like I'm on some crazy voyage, and I don't have a clue where it's going to end. But wherever—I'm on for the ride."

27

The Debarkation Ball took place a week before their departure for MC. The boys were dressed in tuxes, the girls in formal gowns with corsages. Gregor had wanted to wear sneakers as a kind of protest but had decided against the idea. He was trying to keep a low profile, as Dr. Enk had recommended.

Gregor waited backstage with the other Ten to be presented to the guests. Principal Alexander went from boy to boy offering congratulations. Gregor thought he seemed peculiarly somber for such a festive occasion.

"Ah, Gregor," the Principal said when he finally got to him. "So here you are as well!"

Gregor flushed. It seemed a strange thing to say.

"Well, sir—you read out my name."

"So I did, so I did. Your parents must be very proud."

Gregor didn't like Alexander's patronizing attitude.

"In fact, sir, my mother would just as soon I didn't go."

"Is that right?" Alexander stroked his chin thoughtfully.

"I'm sure you don't share that opinion, Gregor."

"I couldn't really say, sir. I've never been to MC."

The Principal continued to look at him with an inscrutable expression, sympathetic but not entirely friendly.

"Women are funny," he confided, tapping Gregor on the shoulder. "As you get older you'll find that they have their own way of looking at things."

Before the dance, Gregor stood to one side of the room, observing. A cluster of guys had gathered on the dance floor, girls hovering at the edges like bees around a compost heap. At the center stood a tall handsome kid whom Gregor recognized immediately.

Gregor had still not met JT, who had received special instruction on his own instead of at the Institute. At seventeen, JT was already six feet, with full square shoulders and a secure, manly expression, with a broad brow, deep set eyes, a straight nose, and a full, smiling mouth.

"Let's go say hi to JT," Babcock said as he passed Gregor. Babcock had placed a white carnation in his lapel and greased his hair back like a young stud in a slick magazine.

"You think he wants to see us?"

"Sure. C'mon, don't be a wuss!"

Gregor watched as Babcock maneuvered to JT's side. JT was the best running back the Pioneers had ever had. He could do things on the field that were amazing—turn, spin, leap, sprint, dodge. It made you proud to see JT run downfield. It reminded you how amazing human beings can be.

Babcock waited by JT's elbow until he had a chance to gain his attention. JT shook his hand while Babcock beamed and said something in a whisper. They talked for a minute, then JT turned in Gregor's direction and looked across the room.

The crowd parted like the Red Sea while JT crossed to where Gregor was standing.

"Hey, man," he said, putting out his hand, "don't stand on ceremony. You're the only one of the guys I haven't met."

Gregor felt himself blushing. Others had gathered to watch.

"So, you ready for the big voyage?" JT was beaming at Gregor as if they were old acquaintances.

"I guess so," Gregor said. "At least I've learned how to drink like a fish."

JT put back his head and laughed.

"That's good!" he said. "Goddamn, we're going to get along fine."

"Gregor's our resident cynic," Babcock said.

Gregor scowled.

"I think of myself as a realist, actually."

"Touché!" JT whooped, punching Babcock on the arm. "I see we'll have to watch ourselves with Greg."

Gregor enjoyed the ball. He danced with Alicia, who certainly thought his selection a big deal.

"It's such an *honor!*" she kept saying. "The only thing I don't like is that you're going away. I'm going to *miss* you!"

"You sound like my mom," he laughed.

"Oh, yeah? Isn't she just so *proud?*"

"Well, sort of," Gregor said. He decided not to go into his mom's opinions with Alicia.

There was quite a bit of drinking behind the teachers' backs, though Gregor suspected the adults looked the other way. The influence of MC, he supposed.

Toward the end of the evening he saw JT huddling in a corner with Babcock, and he went to join them, something he wouldn't ordinarily have done. He had the impression that they hushed their discussion as he approached.

"Hey, buddy," JT said, but it wasn't as friendly as before.

"Whattaya want?" Babcock asked, and suddenly Gregor remembered why he didn't like him.

"He just wants to say hello," JT said. "Isn't that right, big guy?"

Gregor didn't relish being called big guy, especially since he was shorter than the other two.

"You know what we were discussing before you came?" JT said, smiling.

"Yeah," Babcock said. "Before we had the pleasure of your company."

"No," Gregor said. "What were you discussing?"

"Babcock was asking where this institution came from."

"You mean the Golden Ten?"

"Yeah—*us*."

It was a good question. Though they had been instructed on every subject from proper drinking etiquette to the worship of the bull, no one had explained *why* the practice of sending young men to MC had arisen.

"One thing I don't understand," Gregor observed, "is what MC gets out of this."

"Don't you think it's, like, part of diplomacy?" Babcock said.

"I suppose so," Gregor agreed. "Though why they should want to send the so-called *ten best young men* remains unclear. I mean what kind of diplomacy is that?"

"The way I figure it," JT said, "every ten years MC needs a kind of high-octane transfusion. We'll learn their ways, then we can act as a bridge between the two countries. Interpreting one to the other—that sort of thing."

"Maybe," Gregor said.

"Sure," Babcock said. "It's a ticket to the top."

"Or," Gregor said, "the bottom."

The other boys grew silent. They stood looking at Gregor, the muscles in their jaws working. Gregor hadn't meant to say what he had said, it had just popped out.

"What are you trying to say?" Babcock asked. He was standing too close to Gregor, sort of crowding him. Suddenly all three of them had gone slightly pale. "Gregor thinks he's such a genius."

"Is that right?" JT said. "Are you our resident genius?"

"I'm no genius," Gregor said dourly.

"Sure you are," JT continued. "You know what I'm gonna do? I'm gonna call you genius boy."

This was said in a kidding fashion, not unfriendly, but not entirely friendly either.

"Believe me," Babcock said, "the Golden Ten's a ticket to the top. You better be more careful with your tongue, genius boy," he added, "or someone in MC is liable to snip it out."

28

"Thanks for calling me," Richard said.

He was dressed in his chinos and navy blazer. Packaged meat, Gregory thought. Why did adults even *dress* the same?

"Gregory—I'm not your enemy, you know." Richard was looking at Gregory out of his earnest brown eyes.

Gregory chose not to respond.

"You know, we have some things in common," Richard pursued.

"What would those be?"

"Well, your mother, for one. We both want what's best for her—isn't that true?"

"We might not agree on what that is, Richard."

"We might not be as far apart as you imagine. Taking care of her, for example. We both want to make sure that she's safe and happy, isn't that true?"

Gregory didn't answer.

"This burn, for example. You acted great, Gregory. You really looked after her. But what if you hadn't been there? What if you had been away—at college, for example."

"I'm not going to college for another three years."

"That seems like a long time to you, but actually it isn't."

"What's your point, Richard?"

"Just this—that you're not always going to be there to take care of your mom. Have you thought about that?"

"What's to think about?"

"Her happiness—among other things. You care if your mother's happy, don't you?"

"And you are going to make her happy—is that the point?"

"I'd like to try. I'd like to try to make her happy."

Suddenly Gregory was seized by dread. He didn't want to hear what Richard was going to say. He didn't want to hear how Richard was going to make his mother happy.

"Gregory," Richard said. "Your mother and I are thinking of getting married."

Gregory felt himself go white.

"We were going to discuss it with you before your mom got burned," Richard continued, "but this seems as good a time as any. Your mom is still a young woman. She can't live alone for the rest of her life. I want you to try to understand."

"To understand? You want me to understand."

"I'd like us to be friends."

"Friends?" Gregory felt he was going to say something that couldn't be unsaid. That he hated Richard. That he thought he was a joke. That his mother would have to decide between them. But he was afraid. Afraid that if he spoke he would cry. And if he cried he would attack Richard—attack him physically. Would try to knock him down. So instead he turned and walked out of the room.

29

Just before Gregor's departure, his father gave a small party in his honor, just for his aunt and uncle and a few of his parents' friends from his childhood. They sat around the kitchen table pretending to be happy.

Whether on account of his impending departure or not, Gregor had recently been much troubled by dreams, something about some voyage, his motorcycle accident, some cave—he couldn't make it out. At any rate, he would now be glad to be gone.

"Come on, guys," he said to the adults. "This is supposed to be a celebration."

"He's right," his father said. "Let's bring on the cake. Let's make this a party."

"It's only because you're going away from us," his aunt explained. She was a handsome woman, like his mother, but fuller bodied, not so thin and neurotic.

"Here's to Gregor and the other brave boys," his uncle toasted, lifting his glass of inexpensive champagne. "Your country will never forget you!"

They all drank—except his mom. She had threatened to boycott the party and had come only because Gregor had asked her to.

"I don't know what you want from me," his father had said to her. "The boy's happy enough to go."

"Dad's right," Gregor had said. "There's nothing to

do about it now, Mom. They're not going to change the Ten. Besides, I'd look like a wimp if I tried to wriggle out."

"A wimp? Oh, you dear boy!" And she had hugged him to her. "There are many things in this world considerably worse than looking like a wimp."

"I've written to the President," his mother now explained to her sister. "The whole business is a disgrace."

"Margaret doesn't seem to understand," the father confided, turning to the uncle, "that this will set the family up for life. All you're going to do is cause trouble," he said to his wife.

She looked at her husband with contempt.

"Trouble? You're afraid I'll cause trouble? It's a sorry man who won't look after his own son."

And she got up and left the room.

Everybody sat looking at one another in silence.

"She's not herself," the father explained. "This whole thing has thrown her for a loop."

"Give her some time," the aunt said. "After all, Gregor's her only child."

Gregor got up and followed his mother into her room. He could see her lying curled on the bed. And he remembered how as a child he would sit by her in the afternoon while she rested.

"Mama?"

She sat up and reached for him, hugging him to her breast.

"Promise me, Gregor," she said. "Promise me you'll come back!"

He hugged her too, recalling their love, deeper than anything in his life.

"Yes, Mama," he said. "I promise."

After the guests had left, Gregor remained in the kitchen with his father. His father was drying the dishes and had put on an apron to protect his white shirt.

"Dad," Gregor said, "if you know something I don't know about this Golden Ten business, I wish you'd tell me."

His father paused and looked at Gregor.

"What would that be, Gregor? What would I know?"

"I don't know. I just have this feeling that there's something more to be said. Something you grown-ups aren't telling us. I mean, everyone acts as if it's such a privilege to be one of the Ten. But then, after they've congratulated us and everything, they sort of look away."

"I see," his father said.

"Like you," Gregor said. "Just now."

"I'm not looking away, Gregor."

"Then there are these rumors . . ."

"Rumors?"

"About MC."

"Don't listen to rumors," his father said. He continued to dry the dishes, his head down. And Gregor remembered how, when he was a kid, he had loved to watch his father cleaning up in the kitchen. His dad had always liked to work with his hands.

"There are no secrets," his father continued after a while. "It's just—growing up, I suppose. Adults know there's loss involved in growing up, along with celebration."

"Loss?"

"Yes. Sacrifice."

"I see," Gregor said. "What sort of sacrifice?"

"Oh," his father said, "just the usual." He put his hand on Gregor's shoulder. "After a point a man can't protect his child, no matter what your mother thinks. I'm sorry, Gregor. The world's bigger than we are."

Gregor thought his father's explanation was pretty sorry, but he left it at that. He wasn't going to get any more out of him. Whatever the secret—if there was a secret—he wasn't going to pry it out of his father. Or out of any adult.

30

During his last day at the Institute, Gregor started a conversation with the lame boy who worked there. None of the other guys had spoken to the boy, so far as Gregor knew; but Gregor didn't think it right to leave without ever saying a word to him.

He was soon sorry he had.

The boy's name was Alex and he served as a kind of

office boy around the Institute. Gregor stopped him in the quadrangle outside the main building. Crows had perched in a tree and seemed to be watching from across the quadrangle. Gregor could hear their cawing echo against the walls.

"So what are you guys doing here, anyway?" Alex asked.

This was some sort of game; Alex had to know what they were doing.

"We're learning about MC."

"Oh, yeah? Why would you want to do that?"

"We're the Golden Ten!" Gregor exclaimed.

"The Golden Ten!" Alex said. "My, my!"

Gregor didn't like this tone. Without being entirely conscious of it, he had considered himself virtuous in speaking to Alex. Alex was a dwarfish boy, lame in one leg, with sharp, pixielike features, and nervous, intelligent, unfriendly eyes.

"You *do* know about the Golden Ten," Gregor now said, being ironical in his turn.

"The Golden Ten?" Alex said. "You don't mean football?"

"Very funny," Gregor said. "The Golden Ten just happen to be the most gifted guys of their generation." He blushed. Something about this kid goaded him into bragging in a stupid, untypical fashion.

Alex was watching out of cold, ironic green eyes.

"The most gifted guys! Isn't that wonderful. And what, precisely, are *your* gifts?"

"My gifts? What are my gifts?" Gregor repeated, flustered. "Well, I'm very good at—all sorts of things!"

"I'm sure," Alex said.

"And who are you?" Gregor demanded. "What precisely do *you* do?"

"Wouldn't you like to know!" Alex answered with a wave.

"This is ridiculous," Gregor said. "You're just an office boy."

"An office boy!" Alex blanched. "That shows what *you* know. Nothing gets done around here without me."

"I see," Gregor said sarcastically. It was clear why nobody spoke to this kid. He was cracked.

"The Golden Ten," the lame boy spat. "Do *I* know the Golden Ten? I could tell you a thing or two about your Golden Ten, funny boy. If I wanted to."

"What could you tell me?"

"Ah! Now you want to know what little Alex has found out. What do you think I'm doing here, anyway? Why do you think they keep me here?"

"I dunno," Gregor said. He deeply regretted having spoken to this boy.

"You think it's so special to be the Golden Ten," Alex said. "The most gifted guys of your generation! Where are the other Golden Ten—can you tell me that?"

"W . . . what do you mean?"

"From ten years ago? From twenty years ago? If they're so special, why don't you see them?"

This question had bothered Gregor. He assumed the

previous Ten had become hotshots in the Bureaucracy, the government, the diplomatic corps. But why were they never trotted out at banquets? At patriotic events? He had certainly never noticed them.

Alex was watching with amusement.

"Listen, Gregor—that's your name, isn't it?"

"Yeah, that's right."

"Well, it just so happens that my brother was chosen to be one of the Ten a decade ago. He was tall and handsome, great at football and track—a real mama's darling. I remember the excitement. One of the Golden Ten! There was even more nonsense about it back then.

"I recall the day he left. How proud my mother was! He promised to come back—what's wrong, does it sound familiar? Well, off he went with great fanfare, but did he ever come back? Did my golden brother ever return?"

"What are you getting at?"

"He never came back, Gregor boy. *No* one has ever come back. Not a single one of the Golden Ten—*the most gifted guys in their generation.* Wasn't that your phrase? Not a single one has ever returned to the Homecountry."

Gregor felt as if someone had punched him in the stomach.

"How do you know all this?"

"How do I know?" Alex looked at him in triumph. "Well, for one thing, I empty the wastepaper baskets.

You can bet I see all kinds of stuff. Memorandums. In-house papers. Stuff nobody is supposed to see."

"You mean," Gregor exclaimed, "you know this because you empty the *wastepaper* baskets? Jesus, Alex, you can't make allegations like that on the strength of what you find in a wastepaper basket. You're a nutcase, you know that?"

"A nutcase!" Alex's face turned deathly white. "Is that what you think I am? Why do you think I have this job? Why do you think I'm the only kid in the Institute? Because I *know* too much, that's why. They have to keep an eye on me. And I keep an eye on them, believe you me!"

Again Gregor felt an involuntary shudder. This Alex was *creepy*.

"And what do you see?" he asked in spite of himself.

"Oh, I see lots!" Alex looked at him and smiled. "You think the adults don't know where they're sending you? You think they don't know what's involved? Haven't you noticed they're always looking guilty? Always looking away? They know perfectly well what you're in for—you Golden Ten!"

"What are we in for?"

Alex hesitated for a moment.

"I don't know exactly," he admitted. "That's why I'm still here—trying to find out. Trying to find out what happened to my brother."

"Then you can't say for sure that *anything* happened."

"Oh, something happened all right. And someday I'll find out, and then there'll be hell to pay. *You'll* find out soon enough. But *you* won't be coming back to tell!"

31

Gregory sat by the swollen stream. The water threw up glints from the afternoon sun. If he stood he could see the house, though hunkered down like this, he was completely protected from the road.

He had discovered the stream during the first week after they had moved from the old house, and at first he had come here frequently. It was a private spot and the stream ran by with a clear purling sound and you could almost forget that the world was only a hundred yards away. But after the death of his father he had stopped coming.

When he was a child his mom used to take him to the crayfish pond at the end of the lane. The wind was filled with a cool, watery light after the winter. He would stare into the murky pool but he could never see to the bottom. He must have been three years old.

"Not too close, Gregory," his mother would say. "You don't want to fall in."

"But where are the crayfish, Mommy?"

"They hide in the bottom where it's muddy. Maybe you'll be lucky, Gregory. Maybe you'll see one."

But he never did—only the small purple and white

violets that clustered under the dead leaves, the glint of sunlight on the sides of the rocks, the sweet and warmish April that entered his mouth.

But he would never share this spot with his mom. Not now. Let her find her own place with Richard!

He would like to share it with Virginia. To sit with her. Talk with her. See the sun shining in her hair. Why did she have to be in love with Jed? Why did it have to be this way? Stupid!

Gregory tried to think whether this had happened to him before, sitting like this on the bank of the stream listening to the water—but he knew it hadn't. He was alone. No cross-over could ever change that.

Let his mom marry Richard for all he cared. They deserved each other. If she could love Richard after his dad, then he for one didn't want to stick around. *Sayonara,* as Jed liked to say.

His dad! It had all started with his wanting to move away from their old house. Run away! No, move away. (He didn't hold that against him.) And then his not getting the job (Mr. Power!). And then his chickening out. Deserting them. ("He was sick, Gregory. Your dad was no longer emotionally well.") Chickening out and deserting them. And then . . .

POW!

Gregory stood up and began hurling stones into the stream. Soon he was pelting the water as hard as he could, swearing under his breath. And as he swore he heard his father's voice in his ears.

". . . not what you say, son, and not what you believe in this small corner of a universe where we find ourselves surrounded for all time by an infinite expanse of nothing-at-all, but how you behave, and how you treat your fellow man, that is the ultimate measure . . ."

HIGHSOUNDING WORDS!

"You goddamn coward!" he screamed, pelting the stream with stones. "You goddamn son of a bitch!"

And, weeping, he determined to follow the dream wherever it led. Whatever was happening, whatever weird change, mental or actual—how could that nightmare be worse than this?

BOOK TWO

1

The bus terminal was almost deserted when Gregor and his father arrived at 6:45 A.M. The horizon was lit with a band of fluorescent pink across which birds swept in black wedges. The terminal was constructed of poured concrete, the floors stained with dried puddles. Wrappers and newspapers lay strewn in corners; a few old men slept on the plastic scoop chairs, their collars up against the cold.

At the last minute Gregor's mother had refused to come.

"Why the west side *bus* terminal?" she had demanded. "I'm not going to say good-bye to you in that place."

Gregor thought it a little weird himself, but he kept his own counsel.

"They probably prefer to bus the kids out to the airport," his father explained. "The plane is probably leaving from a less conspicuous runway."

"Less conspicuous than *what*?" his mother demanded.

When she embraced him, Gregor feared he would cry.

"Listen, Mom," he said. "I'm going to be all right. I wasn't born yesterday. I don't want to be deaded any more than you want me to be deaded."

It was a joke between them, something he had said as a little boy. And she smiled.

The other boys straggled in to the terminal looking tired and excited. Principal Alexander acted as chaperone. In the general confusion Gregor thought he saw Alex peering out from behind one of the kiosks, but that was impossible, since no one was supposed to know about their departure. When he looked again, he couldn't see anyone.

"Well, Gregor," his father said, "this is *au revoir.*" And he gripped his son's hand.

Gregor remembered the time when he had thought his dad was the greatest guy in the world. He supposed that this change was part of the loss his dad had told him about, the loss that was part of growing up.

His father and he embraced in the dirty hall.

The boys clambered on board an old bus. Most of the seats were empty. Gregor sat by himself and stared out the window at the ugly concrete walls of the terminal. He had a sudden urge to say good-bye to his dad again, but when he looked out the window he had gone. And again he had to struggle not to cry.

"Well," Lewis said, sitting across the aisle. "I guess this is the big day."

"I suppose so."

"Where's JT, anyway?"

"I dunno," Gregor said gloomily. "I guess he'll meet us at the airport."

Then, unlike the boys toward the front, who were

talking in loud, excited voices, they relapsed into silence. Slowly the bus filled with the noxious fumes from the diesel engine.

But the bus didn't stop at the airport. It continued south, bumping along the highway, its motor a constant congested hum, like a large vacuum cleaner. Gregor sat staring out the window, watching the trees and the disappearing city. After a while he dozed off.

As he was leaving the school, Gregory ran into Jed.

"I'll come too," Jed said.

That struck Gregory as a poor idea. Two of them were more likely to get caught leaving school; more likely to get caught breaking into a house and stealing a gun. But Gregory didn't say anything.

They walked down the path to the parking lot. The sun blinked off the windshields of the parked cars. It was hot in the sun though there was a cool breeze.

"We'll take my bike," Jed said.

"You're riding your bike?" Gregory asked.

"Sure."

It was crazy to be riding the bike. Jed had already had his license impounded. But Gregory still didn't say anything.

Jed wheeled the motorcycle backward into the gravel driveway and revved the motor. Gregory swung onto the back. Then they drove out of the parking lot onto the street.

Gregory loved the wind in his hair. The streets flying

by. The freedom. Still, the way Jed did business worried him. It was too much in your face. Sooner or later they'd get caught.

Jed stopped the bike a block from the house and they walked the rest of the distance.

"So what is this place, anyway?" Jed was ambling along as if he hadn't a care in the world.

"The McGruders live here. They've got two kids at school. Mrs. McGruder works, so the place is empty."

"You've really cased the joint."

Now they were approaching the house and Gregory felt his stomach tighten. If he got too nervous he'd get sloppy.

They stood across the street watching the house. Jed didn't seem nervous at all.

"I think it's okay," Gregory said after a while. "We'll walk to the back like we were here to fix something. It's easy to jimmy the back door."

They crossed the McGruders' front lawn. The grass was dead looking from the winter, littered with black, broken sticks like broken antlers. The boys let themselves onto the screened porch and waited to make sure no one was there. Gregory went to the back door and tried to open it with a piece of plastic, but the door wouldn't budge.

Gregor woke with a start, sweating. What was he dreaming? Was it about his motorcycle accident? Where was he? Who were those boys?

Now he could smell the sea—the salty odor of water, the fishy odor of motor oil that floats on the surface of harbors. He didn't like to fall asleep like that. Peering out the bus window, he could see docks and the smokestacks of freighters lining the wharves.

The boys were herded off the bus onto a wharf, where they waited while Principal Alexander consulted with officials. No one paid them the slightest attention. Gregor peered over the side of the dock and saw dead fish floating in the water.

Now Principal Alexander returned and stood talking to a man in a captain's hat and to another man in an old-fashioned gray suit with an umbrella. The man with the umbrella kept squinting at the boys and counting on his fingers.

"You know who that is?" Boyer said in a hoarse whisper.

"No—who's that?" Lewis asked.

"That's the consul from MC."

"Who says?"

"Just look at him. Just look how he's dressed."

Gregor looked, and though he couldn't detect anything unusual about the man, something about him convinced Gregor that Boyer was right. There was something boorish about him, as if he was trying to bully his way out of paying some bill.

"All right, boys," Principal Alexander called. "Come this way."

"Where are we going, anyway?" Furst asked.

"We've decided to send you by boat," Principal Alexander explained. "It will be more expeditious that way."

Expeditious? What did that mean? Gregor thought it meant *fast,* but he couldn't remember for sure. Maybe he didn't have the word right.

But where was JT?

He wasn't going to get onto any goddamn boat unless he saw JT. He had secretly decided that the safest procedure was to stay as close to JT as he could.

They trooped down the wharf carrying their duffels over their shoulders. The consul from MC stood to one side eyeing them suspiciously. He was the first MCer Gregor had ever seen up close, and he looked sinister and weird, with blond thinning hair and temples pressed in as if somebody had caught his head in a vice. His ears were slightly pointy at the top, like a leprechaun's.

Gregor assumed they would embark on the large black ship to their right, with its high sides and ample cabins, but instead they continued to the end of the wharf, where a gangplank ascended to a small dirty oil tanker, low in the water, with two towerlike structures, aft and fore, that served as decks.

"What is this?" Boob laughed.

"Why don't you shut up?" Luck said irritably. He wasn't feeling any happier than Gregor.

Gregor was debating what to do. Should he get onto this tub or not? What would happen if he refused? Then he saw JT waving from the foredeck, and suddenly he felt reassured. Following Babcock, he mounted the gangplank onto the ship.

2

Gregor spent much time topside watching the ocean, whose great swell was broken only by the chop and glitter of the waves. He was mesmerized by the combination of sunlight, loneliness, and a ship far out at sea; he had the strange feeling he had experienced this before. Sometimes dolphins played by the prow of the ship, their backs breaking the water. At night the stars twinkled overhead like distant worlds, dazzling and incomprehensible. Birds perched on the railing, unreasonably far out. And once, curving up in strange grace, a whale appeared and disappeared for twenty minutes on the horizon before departing into the depths.

The ship was rusted, chipped, battered, smelly, small. The crew scrubbed at it constantly (this seemed to be their main occupation), using some raw detergent whose stench sickened Gregor.

Sometimes Gregor caught the crew considering him and the other boys with a kind of furtive curiosity; but mostly they ignored the boys, babbling and chattering to one another in all the known tongues of the globe. The captain was a burly, weather-beaten man who had bowed to the boys and offered a half smile when they boarded the ship, regarding them out of small, blood-shot eyes, after which he said not another word to them for the duration of the voyage.

The Ten ate in the mess with the crew. Gregor could tell what they were serving for breakfast before he reached the mess, and if he inhaled the reek of kippers and coffee he turned away, preferring the morning air; but sometimes as he came toward the galley he'd catch the sweet, yeasty odor of cinnamon buns, and then he'd remember that he hadn't eaten in twenty-four hours.

The cook was a blond young man with an anchor tattoo on his arm. Apparently he was a deaf-mute, for the crew laughed and frowned at him, gesturing with their hands, whereupon he would smile and offer a few incomprehensible grunts.

This sailor had noticed Gregor's partiality for sticky buns, and when they were served, he would keep his eye open, smiling and winking as soon as Gregor entered the mess. Then, wielding his spatula like a baton, he would scoop up three of the fattest buns and slide them onto Gregor's plate.

Once while he was doing this, Gregor observed that the sailor had six fingers on his left hand. Gregor tried not to show surprise, but the cook noticed anyway. He smiled broadly but, Gregor thought, with a kind of menace.

Gregor's bunk lay deep in the hold, next to the boiler room, which hummed and purred night and day, emitting a warm oily smell that bathed everything in a fog. That first week Gregor spent much time lying in his bunk sunk in sleep, troubled by dreams.

3

The boys let themselves onto the McGruders' screened porch and waited to make sure no one was there. Gregory went to the back door and tried to open it with a piece of plastic, but the door wouldn't budge.

"Goddamn!"

"What's wrong?"

"I dunno. The thing isn't opening. I've never had trouble before."

"Let me have a try."

Jed took the plastic and ran it up the inside of the frame, but the door didn't open.

"They've put a dead bolt on," he said.

Gregory took the plastic and ran it above the lock till he felt the bolt.

"They must be on to your little games, Greg-o. Any other doors?"

"Not where we can't be seen. I think we should get out of here."

"Just wait a sec."

Jed took the motorcycle rag from his back pocket and wrapped it around his fist.

"What are you doing?"

"Just watch Uncle Jed."

And he punched through one of the panes on the back door. There was a sound of breaking glass.

"Jesus!"

Jed looked at him and smiled. Then he began removing the pieces of glass from the pane.

"Jed—this isn't a good idea."

"Shh!"

Jed reached through the empty pane where the glass had been removed and drew back the dead bolt. Then he opened the door.

The two boys stood in the darkened kitchen. Gregory's throat was dry. He had never broken into a house before. Never broken a window.

"Jed—maybe we should get out of here."

Jed was examining his hand, making sure it wasn't cut.

"I thought you wanted in," he said.

"Okay," Gregory said. "I'll get the gun and we'll split."

Gregory went upstairs. He couldn't remember whether he had shut the door to the kitchen. Not that it mattered. But it bothered him that he couldn't remember. He was getting flustered.

He entered the bedroom. Light lay on the carpet in a great puddle. Gregory approached the closet and opened the door. He smelled the odor of Mr. Mc-Gruder's suits, lined up like a series of stale ideas. The pistol was on the top shelf in a shoe box.

4

Gregor and Lewis were sitting on the foredeck watching the salty waters dance under the sun. Gregor felt more and more disoriented by the trip and by the confusion of his dreams.

"How long we going to be out here, anyway?" Lewis asked.

"You got me," Gregor said. "No one's told me a thing. Don't you think this boat's a little weird?" he added after a bit. He longed to talk with someone, and he was closest with Lewis.

"Whattaya mean?"

"Well, I dunno. Aren't the Golden Ten supposed to be this big deal? So why do they send us to MC in this pack boat? This *barge*?"

"You mean you don't like our accommodations?"

The two boys laughed over that.

"What have you heard about MC, anyway?" Lewis asked. "You ever heard about their cults?"

"Cults?" Gregor said. "What cults?"

"This ancient system of worship. Like voodoo or something."

Gregor hesitated a moment.

"Didn't Alexander say that all that was in the past?"

"Yeah—I guess."

"So—what are you saying?"

"I dunno. I guess we should forget it. Right?"

Gregor longed to hear more, but something held him back. He didn't want to be subject to every crazy rumor. He didn't want to be spooked.

JT had kept to himself for the first week at sea, but when Gregor returned to his cabin that afternoon, he found JT perched on the edge of his bed.

JT looked great, strong and ready for anything. His face inspired confidence—manly and nice looking, the kind of face people trust.

"So what's up with you guys, anyway?" he asked, and he threw Gregor's pillow across the cabin where it bounced off Fume's chest and landed on the floor.

Everyone laughed—even Gregor, though he wasn't thrilled about having his pillow on the ground. But he wanted to stay in with JT if he could. He stooped over and picked up the pillow. He shared the cabin with Fume, Luck, and Lewis; Fume and Luck on one side, Lewis and himself on the other.

"That yours, Gregor boy?" JT said. "Sorry about that. So, how you guys been amusing yourselves? What's to do on this tub?"

"Diddly-squat," Luck said.

"Oh, yeah? You guys doing calisthenics? You staying in shape?"

"How you supposed to do calisthenics in this place?" Luck asked.

"I'll arrange something," JT said. "I'll have a talk with the Captain."

"The Captain!" Fume said. "What makes you think you can talk to the Captain?"

JT only winked.

Lewis had entered the cabin and was starting up to his bunk, but JT caught him by the arm.

"Where you going?"

"Up to my bunk, JT. Anything wrong?"

"Nothing. Only it's not your bunk anymore. I'm requisitioning that bunk for my own purposes."

Lewis looked at him puzzled.

"What are you talking about?"

"Sleep purposes. Hang out purposes. General jerk off purposes. Okay?"

"JT—that's *my* bunk."

"That's just what I'm saying, Lewis. It isn't yours anymore."

JT said all this with a kind of half smile on his face. It wasn't easy to tell whether he was serious.

"So where am I supposed to go?" Lewis asked.

"I dunno. There must be some hole you can crawl into—right, guys?"

Fume and Luck laughed unpleasantly.

"Very funny," Lewis said. And he started climbing up onto his bunk again.

JT grabbed him by the leg and pulled him down.

"Jesus, JT!" Lewis said. You could see he was pissed. The other boys were laughing.

JT didn't say anything, he just looked at Fume and Luck and smiled.

Lewis started back up, but JT pulled him down again—unceremoniously, so that he landed on the floor.

"Goddamn it!"

"Now, now. Pioneers don't swear."

"I don't get the game, JT."

"No game," JT said. And with a single bound he vaulted onto the top bunk. "This is my bunk—that's all."

"Why don't we take a vote?" Gregor said.

"A vote?" JT looked at Gregor coolly. "What about?"

"About whose bunk it is."

"Brain child over here wants to take a vote," JT said to Luck and Fume. "How are you two guys gonna vote?"

"Not just them," Gregor said. "We'll assemble everybody."

JT considered Gregor from under his brows. "I see," he said. "A regular town meeting. But what if I don't want to hold a town meeting?"

"Well, how are we going to decide then?" Gregor asked. "How are we going to decide important questions?"

"Like what questions?"

"Who knows what's gonna come up."

The other boys were listening closely now.

"Maybe he's right," Luck said. "Not about the bunk or anything. But maybe we should all meet together."

"What for?" JT said.

"Well, I dunno," Luck said. He wasn't looking at JT. "Some of us feel a little, you know—confused."

"There's nothing to be confused about," JT said. He leapt off the bunk.

"Here, Lewis," he said. "You can have your bed. I was just kidding." He went to the door and then, turning, looked at Gregor.

"If you're feeling confused you can come to me. We don't need any idiot town meeting."

5

Gregory stopped at the top of the stairs. He couldn't remember whether he had shut the door to the closet. He stood for a moment, the pistol tucked in his belt, trying to recall. You're getting careless, he thought. Jed makes you careless.

He returned to the room. Everything was quiet. The sun streamed through the curtains. The door to the closet was closed.

When he entered the kitchen Jed was sitting at the counter eating a chicken leg.

"You get it?" he asked, looking up from his meal. He had taken a number of things out of the refrigerator and lined them up.

"Yeah, I got it."

"Cool." Jed took another bite of chicken.

"Let's split, Jed. Before there's trouble."

Jed looked at him casually.

"There's not going to be any trouble. Let's see the gun."

Gregory removed the pistol from his belt and held it out for Jed. Jed walked over and took the pistol. He stuck it in his belt.

"You keeping it?"

"Yeah."

"I think we should leave."

"I haven't finished eating."

Jed went to the refrigerator and opened the door and took out a bowl of macaroni. He left the refrigerator door open.

Gregory closed the refrigerator. He stared out the window into the backyard. "Never keep a pistol around a house," his dad had told him. "More kids get killed in accidents with guns around the house than in all other shooting accidents combined."

"Mrs. McGruder could be back anytime," Gregory said.

"Okay, okay," Jed said. "I'm almost done." He stood up. Gregory could see the muscles in his stomach like a washboard under his T-shirt.

"Listen, Greg-o," Jed said, "you wanted to be *in,* remember?"

Gregory didn't answer.

"It's *cool* the door didn't open," Jed continued. "It's cool we had to break the window. I mean the *real* thing, Greg-o, isn't just breaking into some little bungalow. That's not what we're talking about."

Jed took the pistol out of his belt and considered it, then stuck it back in. He picked up the dish of macaroni. Then he let it drop onto the floor, where it shattered on the tiles. He looked at Gregory.

Gregory didn't say anything.

Jed picked up another dish and let it drop. Then another. They shattered on the floor.

Gregory watched without saying anything. When Jed was through he stood looking at Gregory with amusement.

"Okay," Jed said. "Now we can get out of here."

6

The door to the boiler room was kept locked. Gregor had never observed anyone going in or out, but from the room there issued a constant rumbling grinding pounding throb, like the snores of some immense sleeping beast. These sounds penetrated the boys' dreams, filling them with foreboding.

"I wish that racket would stop," Luck complained. "It gives me nightmares."

"If it stops," Lewis pointed out, "the boat'll drift around out here like a log."

"Sometimes I think that'd be better," Luck replied.

One afternoon when Gregor had gone into the hold to read, he found the boiler room door ajar. He couldn't resist poking his head in.

The room was a cavernlike space in the bottommost part of the ship; beneath its floor descended the fishy seas. Gregor couldn't see anything at first; the smoky air was lit by an owlish light. Metal stairs descended to the boiler, a great chugging monster bristling with pipes, valves, gauges, and circled by a narrow catwalk.

Something about the place fascinated Gregor. Without thinking he swung down the metal stairs to the catwalk and walked partially around the boiler, feeling the narcotic power of the heat.

"Is that you, boy-o?"

Gregor wheeled. A grizzled reddish-haired man was sitting in the shadow of the boiler regarding him out of narrow, unfriendly eyes.

"Oh!" Gregor exclaimed. "I didn't know anyone was here."

"So you thought you'd take the occasion to slip in unnoticed, is that it?"

"I peeked in," Gregor said, "and before I knew it something drew me along."

The old man gave a guffaw.

"Who can resist a boiler room, am I right, boy-o?"

The man laughed with a kind of harsh glee, as if he had said something clever.

"Check that gauge," he barked suddenly.

"W . . . which one?"

"The one right next to you, dummy! Tell me what it reads."

The gauge was so dirty that at first Gregor couldn't make out anything. He wiped the glass with the arm of his shirt, smudging it with grease, then read the dial.

"Good!" the old man pronounced, nodding his head. "Keep an eye on it, lad. If it gets above forty-five, we're cooked!"

Gregor was beginning to suspect that this guy wasn't all right in the head. He had wild, bitter, sparkling gray eyes, a thin, unshaven reddish beard, a torn, dirty T-shirt, and a large Harley-Davidson tattoo on his forearm. He now produced a pint of spirits from his pocket, from which he drank heartily.

"Yes, sir," he continued. "If J. J. O'Quilty isn't on his toes, this ship'll get blown to smithereens. You think the Captain runs the show? Struttin' around like a cork bobbin' on sludge? What good is he if the ship's got no *steam*? Y'ever thought of that? No, youngun. They go marchin' around without a thought to what's underneath, where the *real* life goes on."

"I never thought of it that way," Gregor allowed.

"'Course you haven't. Younguns don't like to think about what goes on underneath. No one does! How you orphans making out, anyway?"

"Orphans?" Gregor said, taken aback.

"That's right," the old man said, spitting. "Aren't you orphans? Well, it makes no matter. We're all orphans, boy-o—don't you know that yet?"

After that Gregor slipped away to the boiler room whenever he could. J. J. O'Quilty seemed to expect his visits. He'd find the door ajar, would slip in and set to work, checking the dials and gauges into whose secrets the old man had inducted him.

He could never tell what mood he'd find O'Quilty in: sometimes irascible and withdrawn, sometimes loquacious and boozy. But the old man possessed a weird sort of power that made Gregor seek him out.

He didn't tell the other boys about his visits; from the first he thought of them as a secret. It was as if he was expecting the strange old man to tell him something important—maybe about the voyage, maybe about life. Something that he had best keep to himself.

7

"All over the floor?" Virginia cried. "All over the floor?" When she laughed she kicked one foot out in front of her, rocking back and forth and clapping her hands.

"All over the floor," Jed confirmed. Which sent the three of them off again.

They were again sitting in Jed's garage while the late afternoon sun lit the jumble of boxes and tools. Gregory

could smell the coolness and the dust that had accu-
mulated. Virginia sat in the middle of the car seat wearing a bright red blouse which she had pushed up above
her elbows; and, with her dark hair and her black eyes,
she looked to Gregory like some brilliant red poppy that
had been left in the midst of that clutter.

"What are *you* laughing about?" Jed ribbed Gregory.
"You weren't exactly thrilled in that kitchen, remember?"

Gregory still laughed, but less hard. The experience
had actually freaked him out.

"What did you do with the gun?" he asked when Jed
had stopped laughing.

"Aw, don't worry about that," Jed said. "A gun can
always come in handy."

"Mr. McGruder's likely to figure out that it's gone,"
Gregory said. "After that stunt with the macaroni."

Jed was still chuckling, but Virginia had stopped
and was listening.

"He'll report the gun to the cops," Gregory said.

Jed let his cheeks balloon for a minute, then blew
out through his mouth. He took a pack of cigarettes
from his pocket and drooped a cigarette from his lip.

"So what's your point, Greg-o?"

"I guess I don't get it," Gregory said. "We break into
a house—okay, fine. We break a window. Then we steal
a gun—that's okay too. Then we trash the kitchen. I
mean, what's that supposed to prove? I'm not against
it necessarily. I just don't get it."

"He's got a point," Virginia observed from where she was sitting on the Chevy seat. "It's a little sloppy."

"Sloppy?" Jed said. You could see it annoyed him. "Sloppy? Don't catch the chickenshits from Greg-o. You don't have to worry about the McGruders. You're never going to hear from the McGruders again. We're splitting, remember?"

"Don't get pissed," Virginia said. "I just mean that Gregory's got a point."

"If you want out," Jed said with disgust, "that's fine with me."

"I wasn't trying to say that," Virginia said. "I just meant—oh, it's not important."

"Okay," Jed said. "Then keep your goddamn mouth shut."

Gregory and Virginia sat in silence. Gregory kept his eyes on the floor.

"So it's agreed," Jed said. "We're going through with it."

The other two only nodded.

"No more chickenshits, right?"

Gregory nodded again, but he kept his eyes down. He hated the way Jed treated Virginia.

8

JT arranged for the boys to do calisthenics on the foredeck, thus demonstrating his influence with the Captain and increasing his prestige even more. The boys were divided into two teams and set a series of competitions and games—playing tag, running relay races, wrestling.

During these exercises Gregor got a good look at JT's daring and agility. He could run back and forth in the roughest of seas, walk the rails, swing out over the edge of the boat. He liked to push the boys beyond their limits: tie ropes to the gunwales and make them swing down to a porthole, or scale the mast in heavy weather. Gregor liked the workouts, though his leg was still stiff from his motorcycle accident of the previous year; but some of the boys were noticeably scared, and once Boob almost fell into the drink.

After dinner they would sit on the foredeck, the boat swaying peacefully under the westerlies.

"Well, here we are," JT said. "Ten little Indian boys!"

"What happened to the Ten little Indian boys, anyway?" Lewis inquired.

JT looked at him with annoyance.

"Don't worry, Lewis—nothing's gonna happen to *us.*"

Stars had pricked out in the sky, and Gregor could see the silver of the moon glittering in a long shaft along the dark swell of the sea. He remembered when long ago he had gone walking at night with his father.

"I wish it could last like this forever," Boyer said wistfully.

"Why's that, Boyer?" JT asked.

"Oh, I dunno. I guess I'm in no hurry to get to MC."

"MC will be fine," JT assured. "A little rough at the edges, maybe—but we'll get used to that. After all, we're Pioneers!"

"Do you know what we'll be doing exactly?" Gregor asked.

"Exactly? No, I don't know exactly," JT admitted. "We'll find out soon enough."

"Is it true," Lewis asked, "that out in the countryside they still have these ceremonies where people get killed by bulls?"

"Who told you that?" JT said.

"I've heard it too," Boyer said after a moment.

"Listen," JT said. "All societies have peculiarities. The Spaniards have bullfights. The Romans had gladiators."

"Yeah—but the Spaniards don't sacrifice the matador to the bull."

JT spat. "That's all nonsense," he said. "Besides, what do we care what they do in the boonies?"

"I care what they do to us," Gregor said.

Everyone grew quiet.

"What is that supposed to mean?" Babcock demanded.

"Yeah," Lemon said. "Sometimes I wonder what you're doing here."

"What are *you* doing here?" Gregor asked.

"I'm a Pioneer," Lemon said, flustered. "And I'm damn proud to be one!"

"That's right," JT said. "I think we all feel that way."

There were murmurs of assent, though less hardy than they might have been.

"Listen," JT said. "Believe me—the Homecountry didn't choose me to come on this mission for nothing. Things are afoot that I'm not at liberty to discuss. But—everything is going to be fine."

JT approached Gregor while he was leaning against the railing looking out to sea. *Ten little Indian boys,* Gregor was thinking, repeating the phrase JT had used.

"So, Gregor boy—what do you see out there?"

"Water."

JT chuckled. The two boys were silent while they watched the vast swaying ocean, beautiful and unfathomable.

"When do you figure we'll get to MC?" Gregor asked.

"Two days." The information was offered as fact rather than opinion.

"You know, Gregor," JT said. "You could help me with the other guys."

"Can I? How can I do that?"

"I don't want you stirring them up," JT said.

Gregor scowled.

"How do I stir them up?"

"The other night, for example. With Lemon. When you asked him what he thought he was doing here. Lemon is proud to be one of the Ten. He believes in what we're doing."

"What *are* we doing?" Gregor asked.

JT studied him for a moment.

"What do the others think we're doing?"

Gregor shrugged.

"They think all sorts of things. Lemon thinks it's the greatest honor since the Olympics. Furst is certain we're all going to be eaten by Bigfoot."

"If you get a guy like Furst riled up," JT said, "he'll spook everybody. That's why I'm asking for your help. Everything's going to be cool, I promise. I'm here to see that nothing happens to anyone."

"You still haven't answered my question—what are we doing here?"

"Between us?"

"Yes—between us."

"Well, we're kind of high-class hostages," JT said.

Gregor felt a wave of fear pass down his spine. He remained staring out to sea.

"We're not going to MC because we *want* to," JT continued. "We're going because MC *demands* it."

"Some *honor*," Gregor said bitterly—and he thought of his mother. "So what happens to us?"

"Nothing. Nothing happens. Only they don't let us go home."

"For like what—fifty years?"

"No—nothing like that. I'm going to put an end to all that. I'm going to renegotiate the whole thing. But I can't if the guys are all panicky. That's where you come in."

"You don't have to worry," Gregor said. "They don't listen to me anyway."

"Maybe they do more than you think. They know you're smart."

"Smart?" Gregor said. "If I'm so smart what am I doing here?"

9

"How long have you been at sea?" Gregor asked J. J. O'Quilty.

They were in the boiler room in the smutty half light illumined now and then by a flare from the molten interior of the boiler. The old man looked at Gregor thoughtfully.

"It seems like about a hundred years."

O'Quilty sat chewing on his pipe while Gregor kept an eye on a quivering gauge.

"You must have seen a lot in your time."

"I guess I've seen just about everything there is to see. Every manner of rascality that man can invent. It's written, sonny, that man's heart is given to evil from the days of his youth."

Gregor digested that for a while. He longed to ask O'Quilty about MC, though he was fearful what the old man might say.

"Do you know where we're headed?" he asked after a pause.

"Yup," O'Quilty said. When the boiler flared it lit the red stubble of the old sailor's beard, giving him an even wilder appearance.

"It's supposed to be a secret," Gregor said after a time.

"A secret!" O'Quilty said with scorn. "What kind of secret do you think they can keep from J. J. O'Quilty?"

"Have you ever been there?" Gregor ventured after a while.

At first the old man didn't answer. He sat pulling on his pipe.

"Feels like I've been just about everywhere," he said finally. "Seen many strange sights. Men who eat bugs. Men who worship cows and bulls. Men who sacrifice boys and girls, like back in pagan days."

"But what do they do where we're going?"

"Can't say what people do behind closed doors."

"You hear queer things about them," Gregor said. "I really don't know what to expect."

"Expect?" the old man said. "Why don't you just expect the worst?"

None of this made Gregor feel any better.

"There's one of them MCers on board right now,"

the old man said. He was smoking his pipe and watching Gregor with a kind of suppressed humor.

Gregor felt a foreboding. "Who?"

"That youngun. The cook with the anchor tattoo."

Gregor realized that he meant the sailor with the six fingers, and for some reason the information made him feel sick.

"I didn't know," he stammered.

The old man remained looking at him.

"I don't believe 'n anything myself," O'Quilty said after a time. "Seen too much of the world. But if I was a believing man, it's that old religion I'd believe in. The pagan gods of darkness, not the newfangled one for children and old maids. That's not a drinking man's religion. This world was made in fire and brimstone, sonny boy. It lives on blood. How do you know I won't trip you up someday and throw you into that furnace?"

Gregor stood staring at the old man.

"Happens every day," the strange old man continued. "Don't believe me if you don't want, you'll find out for yourself soon enough."

"What do you think I should do?" Gregor finally stuttered.

"Do about what?"

"About MC. About *everything.*"

The old man spat.

"Do what you gotter do, sonny. A man's gotter do what he's gotter do."

"But you make life sound like . . . a nightmare," Gregor said.

"A nightmare?" And J. J. O'Quilty chuckled. "Dreams is what's real, sonny! When you're awake, *that's* when you're dreaming. You're nothing but a little dream a piece of dirt is having. A little fleck of mud. Lookee here, like this." And he leaned and picked up a splinter of dirt from the ship's floor. "Then you disappear, poof! You're the dream, boy-o. And dreams—they're what's dreaming *you!*"

10

"Wow!" Gregory said in awe. "You just about killed us!"

The boys sat on the side of a hill in the fresh May air while sunlight rippled the leaves. They could see the hills rising in the distance like the backs of whales, blue and purple on the horizon. The wind tasted of metal.

They had taken the motorcycle into the country, a stupid idea, since Jed's license had been confiscated; but the scheme was set for the next day and they didn't care.

It was one of those afternoons when the air enters your lungs like a drug. Gregory had climbed onto the bike behind Jed, his blood racing.

"I'll go down Falkland," Jed called over his shoulder. "No point driving down the middle of town—some cop'll stop us."

They played hooky now as frequently as they attended school. If Gregory's mom found out there'd be hell to pay, but soon he'd be out of there and there'd be no Mom.

They drove past the university's experimental farm out into the country, Gregory feeling the lurch of power as Jed gunned the motor. The wind licked his hair, his heart leaping in connivance and approval. Now the country was whipping by. Pow Pow Pow! He felt his stomach catapult as they plunged downward over a hill.

"Let 'er go!" Gregory yelled against the roar of the wind.

Both boys crouched down while the wind whistled past them like bullets.

Gregory's laugh caught in his throat, a strange whine that trailed behind him like gauze. When he looked, the road below was racing impossibly fast; he had an impulse to touch it with his foot. They took a curve, and the bike bent like a bow, beautiful and elastic, and Gregory sensed it like a powerful animal beneath him, instinctive and full of grace. This was it! This was IT!

He never saw the hole. Suddenly the bike was sailing through air, he felt the nothingness in his stomach, knowing he was dead. Then they had hit hard and were skidding sideways, Jed braking, and then Gregory was flung upward and never even felt the impact as, tumbling, he came to a stop in mud.

He could see the silence of the sky.

He was alive.

He sat up slowly. Where was he? Where was Jed?

The bike lay on its side on the grassy shoulder, its wheels still spinning.

Then he saw Jed sitting in the gully laughing.

"So that's death," Jed said. They sat on the hill by the side of the road while the wind tussled their hair. "It's nothing at all," Jed said. "Just plain nothing!"

The bike stood below them, dented and muddy but still working. Jed's forearm was badly skinned, but other than that the boys were in one piece.

"A big zero," Gregory said.

"That's right," Jed agreed. "A big ostrich egg."

They grew thoughtful.

"You could do it anytime," Jed said after a while. "Have it all over with. It's as simple as that."

Gregory looked at him.

"Then why are people so afraid?"

"I dunno. People are just plain stupid."

It was true, Gregory thought. You could do it any-time. Like his father. Life, which seemed so solid, was really no more than the spurt of a match. He could have died just then—he wouldn't have felt anything. Just that burst of adrenaline, that excitement—and then, nothing. But then . . . what about his mom? Could he leave her like that? Could he?

He could hear the small crickets in the grass. Smell the earth. Feel the sun on his knees. Life made no sense. None of it made any sense. But could he return to that hurtling instant? That end?

"Do you think there's anything after death?" Gregory asked.

"Well, I dunno." Jed considered thoughtfully. "I read this article in the paper, about people who had died and been brought back to life."

"How is that possible?"

"I dunno. Their heart stops, they're dead—sometimes for minutes, sometimes even longer. Then something happens, someone works on them or something, gives them artificial respiration, and—bingo! They come back to life."

Gregory was dumbfounded. Jed always had some crazy piece of information. He associated what Jed had said with his own dream experiences. What if being dead was to enter that dream world? To enter it forever, without hope of awaking. Without hope of escape. Then reality would be . . . a nightmare!

Gregory felt as if he was being buried alive.

What if what was most wonderful was this now? Being alive. Was that what the dream was trying to say?

The two boys remained silent.

"How does it feel that your old man offed himself?" Jed asked after a while.

Gregory scowled. "How do you think it feels?"

"I think it's sort of cool," Jed said. "I mean isn't that sort of the ultimate high? The ultimate *fuck-you* to the universe?"

Gregory didn't answer. But he knew that his dad's suicide wasn't cool. (He didn't want to see. Didn't want to see the room. The bed. How could he live with this? How? Burned into his brain forever . . . He wanted to shout, that's not what he was like. He was cool! He was great! But what was the point? It was impossible to explain.)

It wasn't cool, what his dad had done. It was (he could barely force himself to think this) a failure. ("He was sick, Gregory, he wasn't well . . .") And it was just like Jed to get this wrong.

11

"I thought we were going to die."

Gregory was sitting next to Virginia on a park bench with the sound of traffic filtering to them through the late afternoon stillness. Cool air rippled the leaves. He watched her wrinkle her brow, her eyebrows drawing almost together.

"You shouldn't go out riding with Jed."

"You sound like my mother."

But she only shrugged.

"Well, maybe your mother's right. How is she, anyway?"

He turned away slightly.

"I dunno. Okay, I suppose. My mom doesn't let on to what she's feeling."

"I like your mom," Virginia announced.

"Whattaya know about my mom?"

"Just what you've told me. But she sounds okay."

Then they both sat contemplating the small park with its few trees and its rusted turnabout with the bent red handle.

"I used to love those things when I was a kid," Virginia said. "I never could get them to go fast enough."

He looked at her, a heady mixture of young lady and daredevil. Someday she would have to choose.

"Maybe *you* shouldn't go out riding with Jed," he said. "Why are you so crazy about him, anyway?"

She looked down, concentrating.

"I dunno. I've asked myself that many times. But I really don't have an answer."

"It's not such a great idea, y'know."

"Liking Jed?"

"Yeah."

She gave a snort.

"Do you think," Gregory continued, "it's because he's like, y'know—trouble?"

She looked at him.

"Is that what you think?"

"That's what I like about him," Gregory admitted. "That he won't eat shit the way everyone else does."

"Exactly!" she said, taking fire. "He won't eat shit. He can't be pushed around! That's so great," she said, "that you see that too."

"Yes—I see it."

"Like my dad," she continued. "He's eaten shit all his life. That's how he's gotten where he is. I used to love him more than anything in the world, can you believe that? We had great times together, me and my dad. We were sort of in cahoots against my mom. She was always flying off the handle, yelling and screaming about something stupid. She could be scary! Dad and I would look at each other behind her back and roll our eyes—you know what I mean? And then everything was okay. Only this is the problem—it turned out my dad was an asshole. He got all uptight if I didn't act like the other kids—if I wanted to be a little different. He acted like that toward Mom too. He tried to control her, that's why she got so mad. At least part of the reason. The truth is, whatever their problem, it bores me. I just want out, y'know? I want my own life."

"I know exactly what you mean," Gregory said. "That's how I feel also. Like my mom now wants to marry this guy Richard. I mean how long has Dad been dead, anyway? Eighteen months? Two years?"

The two sat looking at each other, and he remembered the scene with her mom, her arms flailing, while he crouched outside in the dark.

"You're sweet," she said after a pause.

But he didn't want to be *sweet*.

"I wish," she added, "that we could call the whole scheme off. I have bad vibes about it."

He looked at her, but she was looking away, out toward the street where the cars were passing.

"There's no going back," he said. "We've got to see it through, for better or worse. Like my dreams."

She had turned to listen to him.

"Have you ever thought," he asked, "that the world you dream might be the *real* world?"

"You get the creepiest ideas."

He gave a laugh.

"What if," he said, "there is one universe, far, far away, that is the real universe? The way these archetypes that Richard told me about are real and our dreams are copies of them."

"Yeah? So?"

"So the other universes, the parallel ones I mentioned, might be copies of the real universe, only less and less clear, like planets circling the sun."

"And we're one of these copies?"

"Yes, that's what I think. Only sometimes, in times of crisis maybe, we cross over into these other universes—or they cross over into ours."

"And you think that's what's happening in your dreams?"

"That's what is seems like to me."

He could hear an airplane passing far overhead, its rumble continuing on and on, like some comment you want to ignore but which won't go away.

"You know," he said after a while, "when I was on the

ground, after the accident, I just lay there for a while looking at the sky. It couldn't have lasted long, but for that moment I had this incredibly peaceful feeling, as if everything was okay. I mean I sort of saw how stupid everything is—all the things we worry about and take so seriously, and how good it is just to be alive. I can't really put it in words, because it was all mixed up with this realization about how small we are—just these tiny specks staring up at the sky."

"I think I know what you mean."

"I can't really express it. It was kind of contradictory like—both the meaningless of it all and also the goodness. I think you would have to have been there."

"Yeah—but I think I get it, Gregory. I really do."

"Well," he said, "whatever happens, at least one thing came out of the scheme. At least I met you."

12

As Gregor peered out the window of the speeding car, he saw large empty boulevards lined with pollarded sycamores, their mottled bark the color of army fatigues. It was a steel gray afternoon. Low-lying clouds scudded above the shabby roofs of the city. The stores were shuttered with large metal screens that locked at the sidewalk. Only a few pedestrians passed on the broad streets.

MC! He had seen pictures, but nothing had prepared

him for the reality. It was like some provincial Latin American city. He felt both keyed up and removed, as if in a dream. In fact he had a slight fever.

"The outskirts of Columbia," Dr. Kozinski announced with evident self-satisfaction, turning to face the boys from the front seat. "We'll be there soon."

It was strange to hear MCish, a guttural, difficult tongue with elaborate cases and tenses but a rather crude vocabulary. Though Gregor had learned the language from elementary school, it took his ear time to adjust.

They had docked early that morning, the sun a dull ball on the horizon, and disembarked almost immediately into the cold gray air. Gregor had wanted to say good-bye to O'Quilty, but the boiler room was locked. As he trudged down the splintered wharf, he could hardly tell which of the tubby freighters bobbing on that dirty harbor had been theirs.

Dr. Kozinski, the Foreign Minister, was there to greet them.

"Well, lads, I hope you had a pleasant crossing."

"Fine," JT said, assuming his role as their leader. "It's good to be here."

"President Power couldn't be here to greet you," Dr. Kozinski continued, "but he looks forward to seeing you this evening at a banquet in your honor."

They had climbed into two large, antiquated black limousines; Gregor had positioned himself close to JT; then they had whisked northward toward the capital.

At first Gregor sat with his face pressed to the window trying to take in everything. The low-lying landscape was smudged with oil refineries and large belching smokestacks. After a while the movement of the car almost lulled him to sleep and he sat up with a start, frightened that he had let his guard down so easily. He seemed now to be able to fall asleep anywhere. He would have to be more alert or they would snip out his tongue!

He found he was staring into the ear of Dr. Kozinski, an outsize object festooned with coarse orange hair that cascaded from its inner cavity as if his skull was stuffed with the material. Stranger still, the ear was slightly pointed at the top. Gregor thought the vision repulsive, and he turned away with an involuntary shudder.

Now the limousine rounded a corner and they were entering a more fashionable section of the city, with restaurants and kiosks and people hurrying along the sidewalks. Most seemed to be dressed in drab, utilitarian raincoats and hats.

"The White House!" Dr. Kozinski announced proudly.

Gregor recognized the familiar structure, with its elaborate porticoes, its courtyard, and its minaret pointing toward the sky.

They pulled up in front of the Hillcrest Hotel with the flags of the empire, including that of the Homecountry, fluttering above its doors. The boys poured out onto the sidewalk, where they were met by a small crowd of officials and government personnel, including the hotel manager.

The lobby was plush red, with wooden paneling on the walls and large potted palms in the corners. "No need to register," the manager assured. "That's all been attended to."

"Well, lads," Dr. Kozinski said in parting, "wash up, take a little nap, look around the hotel. You can order anything you want at the restaurant—it's on the house. Only I must ask you not to leave the premises. You might be needed at a moment's notice."

"I'm going to get some food," Babcock said. "I feel as if I haven't eaten in three months."

"Yeah," Lemon agreed. "Civilization!"

The hotel manager led them into a private dining room—"where you won't be disturbed," he explained. The boys sat at a long table with a blue-checked table-cloth—Gregor noted it was frayed at the edges.

"What will you have, boys? Perhaps some soup? A nice stuffed cabbage?"

"I'd prefer a hamburger," Fume said.

"A hamburger? I'll have to see if we have any. In the meanwhile I'll have the waiter bring you radishes and celery. And of course some rolls!"

"Don't these guys have *hamburgers*?" Fume asked when they were alone.

"We didn't come here for hamburgers," JT said. "Just mind your p's and q's and don't worry about your stomach."

There were no hamburgers, but the manager did provide a steak—a bit stringy but better than anything they'd had aboard ship. The rolls were stale but the beer was plentiful, and soon everyone was feeling better.

While they ate, people came to the doors and peered in at them as if at some curiosity. Gregor could hear the sound of people eating in the next room, though the doors had been locked between them. He also noticed people craning their necks to see them through the windows.

"Okay, guys," JT said. "Let's get our ducks in a row."

The boys leaned forward attentively.

"I want you guys on your best behavior," JT said. "Don't forget we're representing the Homecountry. We should feel damned honored that President Power is taking the time to meet us this evening. So I don't want anyone blowing it. The next couple of days will be ceremonial, with banquets and stuff. Anyone who learns anything important, report it to me. Otherwise stay cool. Now I suggest we go to our rooms and get some sleep. If anyone wants to poke around the hotel, fine— but don't forget, Kozinski doesn't want us to leave."

Gregor stayed behind. He was running a low-grade fever and feared that if he lay down he wouldn't be able to get up again.

The hotel was constructed around a large central courtyard with a tea garden and small orchestra. Gregor circled the restaurant with its wicker chairs and potted palms, its wrought-iron tables with stout, middle-aged ladies dressed in the fashion of a decade ago, sipping tea. The orchestra consisted of a conductor and half a dozen sleazy-looking performers playing Viennese waltzes. Gregor was surprised to note that, like Dr. Kozinski's, the conductor's ears were strangely outsize, with elongated lobes and slightly pointed tops.

Gregor wanted a little fresh air to clear his head and to still the unease that had gripped him, but when he reached the front lobby, soldiers were posted at the door.

He searched for a side exit, but here too a soldier was on guard. Should he try to walk by? Prudence, however, won out. It wouldn't do to get tangled with the authorities within the first hour of his arrival. He remembered Professor Enk's caution about keeping a low profile.

When he got off the elevator onto his floor, the long corridor was empty. The carpet looked stained and threadbare, the walls dark, with only a few flickering lights. The brass numbers had fallen off some of the doors and been daubed in with charcoal.

Halfway down the corridor a young chambermaid appeared from a door marked Room Service. She was skinny and sallow but smiled at Gregor in a friendly manner as she passed.

"Wait a minute," Gregor called, hearing his own MCish accent as he spoke.

The maid stopped and turned, though she didn't approach.

"Why can't you leave this hotel? Why are their soldiers posted at the doors?"

"I suppose because of the boys, sir." And she giggled.

"Why because of the boys? What's it have to do with them?"

"I really couldn't say, sir. You know how it is."

"Aren't there any other guests on this floor?"

"No, sir. Just the boys in suite 401."

He thought she gave him a peculiar glance, part curiosity, part coquettishness, and part—was it fear? He wanted to ask her other questions, but before he could formulate them she had turned and scurried away.

"Do you know," Gregor said to JT, "that there are soldiers posted at the doors?"

JT had requisitioned a small partition, separated from the rest of the room by a thin wall. He was now sitting on the side of his bed polishing his shoes while the other boys slept.

"Do you think that's normal?" Gregor demanded. "I mean to guard the entrance and exit to a hotel?"

"Who's to say what's normal over here?" JT observed.

"Well, I'm not used to seeing soldiers in the middle of hotels. What's more, there are no other guests on this floor. Just us."

JT studied him while continuing his polishing.

"Who is this Dr. Kozinski, anyway?" Gregor asked.

"He's some big mucky-muck. The Foreign Minister and a personal adviser to the President."

"Did you notice his ears?"

"I wouldn't mention his ears if I were you, Greg-o."

"Oh, yeah. A sensitive subject over here, huh? You should see the conductor in the restaurant. He looks like Leonard Nimoy."

"Gregor-boy—I thought you were going to be on my side."

"Which side is that, JT? I didn't like the looks of that Dr. Kozinski. I don't like the soldiers at the door. I don't like the whole thing."

"Keep your voice down, will you? You want to wake the other guys?"

"I will wake them, JT—unless you tell me exactly what's up."

The two boys exchanged a long stare.

"Okay," JT said finally. "I'll tell you what I know. But only on the condition that you keep your mouth shut."

"Spill it," Gregor said.

"The Homecountry wants to put an end to this tribute business," JT said. "This Golden Ten. That's what I'm doing here."

Gregor felt a shiver run down his spine.

"I'm going to be contacted," JT pursued. "By somebody important. I'm not at liberty to tell you who. Then we'll figure out how to put an end to this. How to get us out of here. But until I'm contacted, we just have to sit tight—get it?"

"And what about me?" Gregor demanded. "Where do I fit in all of this? What am I doing here?"

"Damned if I know." JT shrugged. "I wouldn't have selected you myself—but nobody asked me."

"I wouldn't have selected me either," Gregor said. "I don't make any sense as one of the Golden Ten."

"Maybe that's why they selected you," JT suggested. "Maybe because you're different. Maybe because you won't just fit in."

13

At eight that evening the boys were busy scrubbing faces, polishing shoes, straightening ties—preparing for the banquet.

Gregor had rested, but when he got up he felt shivery, his throat dry, his head pounding. He had dreamt again about his motorcycle accident of the previous year. He knew he had to keep his wits about him, he couldn't afford to be ill.

Luck picked up the telephone for room service, but the phone was dead.

"The damn telephone doesn't work."

JT picked up the receiver and listened, but after a moment he put it down.

"There's no ice either," Boyer called. "Plenty of Pepsi but no ice."

"There's an ice machine down the corridor," Gregor

volunteered. "I'll go take a look." He was already dressed and wanted to get away from the other boys.

He took the ice bucket, an oval urn that looked as if it contained someone's ashes, and went out the door.

The corridor was even drearier than before; another light must have burned out. The place smelled of stale food, stale dust, stale humans. The silence oppressed him.

There was no ice in the ice machine.

Coming out of the door, Gregor almost bumped into the young chambermaid whom he had seen before.

She blushed deeply.

"I was trying to get some ice," he explained.

"Oh, that machine doesn't work," she said with a giggle. "None of the machines work."

"What's wrong with this place?" he demanded.

"You must be new around here."

"I just arrived today."

She looked at him ironically for a moment, as if he had said something ridiculous.

"I'll try to get you some ice," she said after a pause. "Where are you staying?"

"In suite 401."

"Oh!" She was taken aback. "I see."

"Why do you say it like that?"

"Like what?" She was more guarded now. Defensive, he thought.

"I dunno. Like you were surprised."

"I thought you were—just visiting. I don't know why."

"Well, I'm not. That's my room."

"Then you must be one of . . . the boys."

"The boys?"

"Yes. For the Great Bull."

He felt a shiver of alarm.

"I'm sorry," she said. She was now definitely scared. "I have to go."

"No, stop. Explain what you mean."

"No, I must—really."

"But just one minute. Tell me what you were talking about."

"No, no," she said. And she scurried down the corridor. But she paused for a moment when she got to the end, and he thought she waved. Then she disappeared.

14

President Power was a tall gangly man with large hands and long ears and a loud booming voice. He greeted the boys with expansive good humor, like a coach at a football conference.

"So these are the Golden Ten! Gall darn it, a fine-lookin' bunch of young roughnecks if ever I saw 'em. So, son (pumping JT's hand), how are your accommodations? Any complaints? If there're any problems, you tell 'em they'll have to deal with the top dog himself—right?"

He slapped JT on the back with considerable force. JT smiled and shook the President's hand and assured him that their accommodations were fine.

"We want you to feel at home here in MC—isn't that right, Kozinski?"

"That's right, Mr. President. Exactly as you say."

"You see what kind of yes-men I have workin' for me?" Power said, turning back to JT. "How can you boys feel at home when you're ten thousand miles from your daddies? I'm surrounded by dolts, that's why I need you boys. Here, Groober," he called to an aide who stood close by. "Give this boy a drink."

And he swooped the glass out of Groober's hand and gave it to JT.

It came to Gregor that maybe President Power was himself the Great Bull. He behaved something like a bull.

The boys were placed at the head of a long table with the President and Dr. Kozinski. Gregor was seated toward the end of the line, next to a dwarfish man with earnest brown eyes and a slight mustache, who turned out to be the Secretary of Education.

The meal began with the Senate chaplain saying grace. He covered his head with a hood, then held up a knife. Everyone bowed his head. Then the chaplain sprinkled a ceremonial platter with a red liquid.

"I hope you boys will enjoy your stay with us," the Secretary of Education said after the benediction. "I'm a great admirer of your country and have worked hard for smoother relations. I think we've made great strides under President Power."

Gregor allowed as how the Homecountry had the highest regard for MC and its President.

"It must be an interesting job," he ventured, "being Secretary of Education."

"Oh, indeed," the dwarfish man agreed. "I have to read every textbook to make sure it doesn't contain malicious scandal about MC and its history. The welfare of our young minds rests in my hands."

"What kind of scandal?"

"Oh, about the Bomb, for example. The most outrageous allegations are leveled against our great country. I would hardly dare tell you what one hears. But that's always the price of greatness, isn't it? Petty minds tell petty tales. You have to keep your eye on the big picture, how things will appear in a hundred years."

"I see," Gregor said.

"I hope you boys will take the opportunity to see our great land as it really is," the Secretary pursued, "from sea to shining sea. Of course some areas are closed to visitors, but that still leaves thousands and thousands of miles! I don't know what exactly is planned for you," he added. Then suddenly he stopped in mid-sentence, as if he had remembered something, and turned noticeably red. "Now wait a minute," he continued. "Let me see. Oh, well, at any rate." And then he turned back to his salad.

President Power rose from his chair at the head of the table. He had a sad bloodhound's face with long creases down his cheeks, his ears hung down like empty pockets, but his eyes were bright, suspicious, watchful, and his mouth curled up into a half smile at the side.

"Now, y'all, we've got a passel of special guests tonight—not just the usual riffraff (laughter), so be on your best behavior—and that goes for you, Kozinski! (More laughter.) These boys have traveled the high seas to be with us, have braved seasickness, homesickness, and I-don't-know-what kind of sickness to pay their respects to our great nation—the greatest goddamn nation on the face of the earth! (Wild applause.) So I know y'all will want to extend to them the welcome they deserve.

"Now I want to share with you something that befell me recently—something that some of you have wondered about and some of you have speculated about but which goddamn few of you have had the balls to ask me about. I mean my recent visit with the surgeons. Now, I'm not gonna pussyfoot around, that's not my nature and that's not the nature of this great country— the greatest country in the world, no, goddamn it, the greatest country the world has ever seen! (More applause, even more enthusiastic.) Well, sir, you ask about my operation? Let me show you!"

And with that he pulled up his shirt and yanked down his pants, revealing a large red scar, a crimson cicatrix on his belly, which started low on his abdomen and zigzagged up to his rib cage.

The entire room was dumbstruck. Finally, half rising, Dr. Kozinski broke into applause. Soon the rest of the room was applauding too, laughing and shouting, so that the entire banquet hall resounded to the ruckus. President Power remained standing, his large hairy belly exposed, his face set in a triumphal smile.

After dessert a singer crooned French songs in a heavy MCish accent. Dancing girls performed the can-can. A magician drew colored silks from the nostrils of the guests (much laughter and applause). Then he released a green dove from the seat of his own pants (hysterical laughter).

Gregor had hoped his fever would subside, but instead he was feeling less and less well. The banquet hall seemed to spin before his eyes. Now he could no longer be certain whether the Minister of Education was actually a man. Maybe he was mistaken, maybe he was a dwarfish woman! Could that be? Or was his fever making him see things?

Before he could decide, the meal ended, everyone stood up, men lit cigars, waiters scurried about serving brandy in large snifters, the guests wandered between tables exchanging words and slapping one another on the shoulder. Some bumped into chairs, others slumped over in corners. When Gregor looked for the Minister, he (or was it she?) was gone.

Gregor made his way through the crowd to where JT was sitting.

"There's something fishy going on here, JT. I think the man I was sitting next to was a woman."

"Are you kidding me?" JT said with a laugh. "He didn't look like a woman from here. You're spooking yourself, Greg-o. You'll give yourself nightmares."

Gregor sat biting his lip. Was he spooking himself? How much could he trust JT, anyway?

"I think I'm coming down with the flu," he confided.

"Oh, yeah? Better go back to the room and get some shut-eye."

"Do you know anything about some Great Bull?" Gregor asked.

"Great Bull?" JT looked at him again. "Where'd you hear that?"

"The chambermaid at the hotel asked me whether I was one of the boys for the Great Bull."

"The great bullshit, you mean," JT scoffed.

"She seemed afraid."

The two boys looked at each other without saying anything.

"Well," JT muttered after a bit, "don't go spooking everybody with your damn nerves. Don't worry, whatever this Great Bull is, I'll get to the bottom of it."

15

When they looked out the window the next morning, a thin gray snow was fluttering noiselessly over the vast run-down metropolis. The roofs stretched to the horizon like rows of old tin boxes. There was little heat in the room, and Gregor shivered against the cold. He was still running a fever.

Gregor, who had again been troubled all night by dreams, was tired, irritable, unwell. In his feverish state it was increasingly difficult for him to distinguish what was real from what was nightmare.

"There's no goddamn hot water," Fume announced, returning from the bathroom with a towel about his waist. "Anyone who wants a shower will have to take it cold."

"When I got up in the middle of the night," Babcock said, "the door to the room was locked."

The other boys looked at him.

"So they locked the door," JT said. "Big deal. Obviously they don't want us getting lost. Now finish up, we've got things to do."

That morning was spent visiting the Senate, where a debate was in progress concerning capital punishment. Public executions were still practiced in the backcountry, and the senators were debating the various merits of rope, guillotine, or bullet.

Afterward they visited Senator Iky's private chambers, where they received autographed pictures of the Senator with his mother.

"It's an honor to meet you boys," Senator Iky said, shaking each of the Ten by hand. "I'm a great admirer of your brave little country. I count you boys as great patriots—of our country as well as your own. *Dulce et decorum pro patria,* and all that."

While this was going on, Gregor noted a kind of altar in the corner of the Senator's office, with the picture of a bull engraved on its side. He wanted to ask Iky about the object, but he was ushered out of the room before there was time.

Luncheon was served in the White House under the auspices of President Power himself: guacamole, fried chicken, heaps of potato salad, and beer. The President said grace, sprinkling the requisite red liquid. Then, while they ate, he recounted stories—many of them off-color—from his own career while stuffing his mouth with chicken and feeding choice pieces to his two basset hounds, who whined noisily under the table.

While the waiter was serving him a basket of taco chips, Gregor noticed that the man's hands were covered with tiny scales, greenish and overlapping, like the back of a lizard. Gregor rubbed his eyes, but the man had already moved away.

Toward the end of the meal the conversation was interrupted by the sound of chanting from outside the window. A guard whispered something to the President, whereupon he rose and, bidding the boys follow him, crossed to the large French windows that gave onto White House Square.

Gregor stepped onto the balcony and beheld a sea of humanity dressed in overcoats and wool hats against the cold. A roar went up when the boys appeared.

"They've come to welcome you," President Power said, smiling out of the corner of his mouth. "The good folk of Mother Country showing their appreciation. A spontaneous demonstration," he added, and his mouth pulled up at the side as if in amusement.

Gregor made out unshaven faces wrinkled with premature age. Teeth were missing, slaver drooled from lips, a kind of taunting, rattling hoot issued from their throats. Some leered, some jeered, some cheered a Bronx cheer, a few raised fists in a strange menacing gesture. Soldiers with guns and bayonets pushed the crowd forward, hindering people from departing. Again a cheer went up, booming and unsettling, as at a stadium when the other team misses a goal.

The final event of the day was cocktails in the basement of the White House. The boys stood on line shaking hands with three hundred guests. Gregor was now running a high fever. It seemed to him that one of the dignitaries had small horns at the back of his head, but when he looked for the man, he could no longer find him.

"Is something crazy around here?" he asked Lewis when the boys had a moment to relax. "Or is it me?"

"I don't know," Lewis said, "but they sure are a bunch of rednecks. It's worse than I expected."

"Haven't you noticed anything strange?"

"Everything's strange," Lewis said.

They couldn't speak anymore, they had to return to shaking hands. But later Lewis caught him again for a moment.

"Have you seen Power's daughter?" he asked.

"No—is she strange?"

"No, that's the point. She's the only one around here who isn't." And he pointed across the room.

Gregor saw a young woman conversing with JT, frowning slightly as she spoke. She was exotic looking, sort of Egyptian, with dark hair and large dark eyes, which she highlighted with eyeliner. Her wrists were delicate, and she had long arms and long tapering hands that snapped up when she talked like lively little animals.

"What's her name?" Gregor asked.

"Ariadne," Lewis said. "JT met her last year when she visited the Homecountry with her dad."

Gregor kept staring at her across the room. He thought she was strikingly good-looking, but he also had the strange, unsettling feeling that he had seen her somewhere before.

Back at the hotel, some of the other guys stayed up trading impressions or chewing the fat, but Gregor, whose head was pounding, sunk down on his bed. Perhaps with a good night's sleep he could fight off the flu. The instant his head touched the pillow, he was sucked into unconsciousness.

He awoke with a jolt in the dark and for a moment he had no idea where he was. He seemed entombed in darkness. His fever had climbed. He couldn't tell how long he had slept. Images from the previous two days wheeled through his head: Dr. Kozinski, the chambermaid, the waiter with scales, the scar on President Power's stomach, the man with horns, JT squinting with warning, the image of the bull on the side of the altar, the sprinkling of wine (or was it blood!) onto the food, Ariadne, the President's beautiful daughter . . .

"Under the Senate," someone close by was whispering. Gregor lay silent, listening.

"What should we do?"

That was JT—and he was whispering to some girl. They must be on the other side of the partition, where JT slept.

"You'll have to kill it yourself," the girl said. "I'll help you. Then you'll take me away—like you promised."

"Yes," JT said. "Yes. Only keep your voice down."

Gregor struggled up in his bed, straining to hear.

"It's some beast," the girl explained. "Some terrible monster. No one talks about it."

Despite his fever, Gregor felt himself go cold. He strained all his faculties, but all he could make out was a hum, as of water gurgling and running together. He lay in a cold sweat, trying to think. He was getting toward the center of the nightmare.

After a while he could hear them moving about on the other side of the partition. She must be getting up, preparing to go. Then he could hear her again.

"I don't care if he's my father," she said. "I hate him. They'll kill all of you! Like that." And she snapped her fingers. "For the sake of their precious Mother Country."

The President's daughter! Ariadne, whom he had seen at the party that afternoon. She must have let herself into their room in the middle of the night.

He tried to get up to confront JT, but his head was whirling. He lay down for an instant, and he felt himself being sucked into a feverish whirlpool. And all the time he was thinking: Monster! Sacrifice! Blood!

Jed and Gregory hid in the boiler room while the other kids left school for the day.

"Not much to worry about," Jed explained. "The old janitor's a pain but senile. He checks the school at six and nine, after that he sleeps till morning. We'll have to hide until everyone clears out of the Emerald Building across town."

Gregory had seen the janitor a couple of times as he came into school, a thin, unshaved, wild-eyed, reddish-haired old man in a torn, dirty T-shirt, with a Harley-Davidson tattoo on his forearm. Something about him always gave Gregory the spooks.

"Does he carry a gun?"

" 'Course not," Jed said. "He's just a stupid old drunk."

They settled down behind the boiler where it was warm and they were hidden from sight. The boiler itself was a great chugging monster bristling with pipes, valves, gauges, from which there issued a constant rumbling grinding pounding throb, like the snore of some immense sleeping beast.

"Now it's up to us, ol' buddy," Jed said. "Just like two orphans lost in the wide world. From now on we're on our own."

Gregory leaned against the wall. Once he would have wanted nothing more than to be Jed's buddy, but now he was less sure. He had never thought there would be a time when he would leave his mother. But, he reflected, he wasn't really leaving her—she was abandoning him. We're all orphans, it popped into his head. Sooner or later everyone is an orphan.

Gregory closed his eyes. Warmed by the heat from the boiler, he fell asleep immediately.

. . . get up Get Up GET UP!"

awoke and saw Dr. Kozinski standing over him shaking him by the arm. Gregor was lying in his bed in the hotel room, though it took him a few minutes to understand where he was. He felt sweaty and weak.

"What happened?"

"You've been ill. Quite a high fever, actually."

Gregor tried to sit up, but his head was dizzy and he sank back onto the pillow. What had he been dreaming? He couldn't make it out.

"How long have I been this way?"

"I couldn't say. It was touch-and-go for a while. You gave us quite a scare."

Gregor tried to recall. He remembered the boat, the first night in the hotel, the banquet and conversation with JT. Everything was dreamlike and hazy. Had someone been in the room with them? Had he overheard some conversation?

"You've got to get up and get dressed," Dr. Kozinski urged. "Today's the day."

The day? Gregor didn't know what he was referring to. He tried to look at Dr. Kozinski but everything swam before his eyes. Did Kozinski have horns, or was he imagining things again?

In the meantime Dr. Kozinski was pulling him out of bed.

Gregor allowed himself to be dragged up though he felt weak. But he shook Dr. Kozinski off when the latter started to undo his pajama top.

"I'll do it myself."

"Well, hurry, then. The ceremony will be starting soon."

"What ceremony?" Gregor slipped into his clothes. He wished there was time to eat something.

"I haven't time to explain."

Dr. Kozinski said this with reproach, as if Gregor's illness was a moral delinquency. Gregor couldn't get his thoughts in order. He was being rushed along, yet he had a weird sensation that he was moving through a dream that had happened before—perhaps many times before. If only he exerted himself he could make it stop.

I'm still not well, he thought. I'll have to watch myself or I'll commit some stupid blunder.

Dr. Kozinski hurried him out into the corridor. For a moment Gregor had to stand still with his hand against the wall to regain his balance.

"Come along, come along," Dr. Kozinski urged.

Gregor thought he saw the chambermaid watching from down the corridor. He closed his eyes, but when he opened them she was gone.

"I'm okay now," he said as he followed Dr. Kozinski to the elevator. "Where are the other guys?"

"They're waiting in the chapel. I don't have time to explain, we're late already."

Dr. Kozinski's words sent a shiver down Gregor's spine. He half considered using some of the self-defense he had learned at the Institute to fell Dr. Kozinski with a blow to the neck—but then what?

The elevator door slid open and he was hurried into a basement where armed guards stood at attention with rifles at their shoulders. Gregor tried to focus his mind but he was being rushed so fast that he couldn't concentrate. Then a large iron door was hurled open and Gregor felt himself shoved so that he staggered forward into the dark.

. . .

"Get up, Narco. Jesus, you really can sleep anywhere!"

Gregory didn't know where he was. He lay trying to re-member the dream, trying to catch it as it disappeared. Some voice was speaking in his head. It seemed com-pletely real while you were in the dream, and now he could hardly remember. Maybe he was in a dream now—how could he be certain? Maybe you could never escape from the world of dreams. And he shuddered with dis-taste.

Jed stood over him, prodding him to wake up.

Gregory sat up slowly, still disoriented.

It was time to enter the Tombs.

The tunnel descended for about ten yards. The space was hot and dirty; pipes ran along the ceiling. A series of unshaded bulbs lit the dark. The boys had to be careful not to hit their heads. At first the tunnel was broad—maybe five feet across—but after twenty yards it narrowed and the lights ceased. The passage split in many directions.

"Now what?" Gregory asked.

Jed took out his flashlight and drew a piece of paper from his back pocket, which he consulted with care. The beam from the flashlight flickered on his face. The tunnels had been built decades ago to provide for un-derground piping and electricity when the municipality was expanding. They fanned out in all directions, criss-crossing the town.

"Here—this way." And he led off to the right.

As soon as he entered the tunnels, Gregory was seized by a sense of suffocation, as if he was being buried alive. This was a cross-over place if ever there had been one, worse even than the basement in his old house. If he wasn't careful he'd never get out.

The Tombs smelled of earth, moisture, stale air. He was shaken by the old sense of familiarity, as if he had been here before. He had to lean against a wall and rest. He had broken into a cold sweat.

Jed turned and looked at him impatiently.

"What's wrong, Greg-o? Claustrophobia?" He smiled ironically.

"I'm all right."

Gregory clenched his teeth. He was determined to stay up with Jed. Already the sense of fear—and of familiarity—were fading. But not the conviction that he was very close to something, some revelation, some understanding.

He pressed forward.

Now he couldn't see—just shadows and looming darkness. The beam from Jed's flashlight shifted and dodged. It cut strange patterns against the wall. He could hear Jed breathing.

He could understand why they called this the Tombs. It was like being in some mummy encasement. His clothing stuck to him in the heat. Sometimes they could stand, amid flickering eerie light, with puddles of water and cobwebs hanging from the roof; at others it was so narrow that they had to walk single file, bent over, with their hands feeling the sides of the walls. Often Gregory had to keep his head down or he would bump it against the roof of the tunnel.

The two boys continued in silence for forty minutes, twisting and turning, stumbling. It was hot and wet and cramped, and for long stretches the only noise was the sound of their breathing. Finally Jed came to a stop.

"Damn!"

"What's wrong?"

"I'm not sure where we are."

"Great!"

"Just keep your pants on."

Jed leaned against the wall, training his light onto the paper. Gregory could see the perspiration on his face. His own heart was beating. If the flashlight failed they would never find their way out.

"Okay," Jed said. "We'll have to backtrack. We should have turned left."

Then again there was silence. Flecks of dust dislodged from the ceiling, got down Gregory's collar, prickled his skin. Once something got into his eye. He had to concentrate not to panic.

Finally they reached the dividing wall; they couldn't go any farther. They sank down, their knees pulled up. The silence whistled in Gregory's ears. And they still had to find their way out again.

"This is your parallel universe," Jed observed.

"Yeah, great. A big black hole."

The metal door slammed behind Gregor with the rattle of closing bolts. He was aware of shadows, dim lights, the pervading odor of candles, a low murmur of voices. Then someone pulled him down into a pew.

"Shhh!"

It was Lewis.

Gregor sat still until his eyes slowly adjusted. He was in a small concrete bunker with reddish lights on the walls. The boys were huddled together in what looked like baggy convicts' uniforms. There was a small wooden door to the front, an altar next to the door. And, mounted above the altar, the head of an immense, horned bull.

"I hoped you wouldn't show," Lewis murmured. "I hoped you'd gotten away."

"What are they up to?"

"Nothing good!"

A man rose from the front pew—Gregor recognized the chaplain from the banquet. He was dressed in a long monk's frock, with a large cowl pulled over his head. He stepped to the altar.

"Holy, holy, holy! Holy is the God of Blood. Holy those who worship Him. Who give offering, who give thanksgiving, who give sacrifice. Holy who keep faith, who keep time and place, who keep word. Holy those who offer the unstoppable stream."

"Jesus!" Gregor whispered.

"Such," continued the priest, "is darkness, such is blackness, such is night. Worship the Bull that holds the night. Worship the Great Bull that holds creation. *He hath graven his name within the hills, and His vengeance be upon the dust within the rock.*"

Boob stood by the altar, his shoulders rounded, his large eyes watching hopelessly. Gregor's heart thumped. In a flash the priest had drawn a knife—and slit Boob's throat from ear to ear so that his life blood gushed onto the floor.

Gregor reeled. Fear pounded in his veins. JT leapt to his feet. Others screamed. Boob's body slumped down into its own blood and lay in a heap. But already soldiers were pushing the boys forward, pricking them with bayonets, herding them through the small door by the side of the altar.

Gregor stumbled through the door and fell. He smelled earth and wet stone—the odor of dungeons. He heard the door slam behind him. He lay on the ground terrified, writhing in anguish. Only now did he realize that he was weeping.

"Okay," Jed said. "Let's see if you can fit through."

Gregory opened his eyes and looked around. Jed was playing his light against the top of the wall. There was only a little creep hole where the pipes ran.

"You think you can make it?"

"I dunno."

Gregory stood up unsteadily. Jed put his hands together and hoisted Gregory up. The pipes were warm but not hot. Gregory lifted his body until he was clinging like a raccoon, his back horizontal to the floor.

"You got it?"

"Yeah, I think so."

Gregory shinnied forward, his chest pressed to the pipes. His head made contact with the opening. If he could get his head through he would be all right.

"Good boy," Jed said.

Now Gregory was halfway through. It was pitch dark. His hips negotiated the passage, and for a moment he thought he was stuck. He felt a wave of panic, as if he might be stuck forever. He thought of his father (he didn't want to see the room, the bed where his father lay sprawled, the fingers part open, limp, didn't want to imagine other things, worse things); then he had wriggled free and swung down, holding the pipes for an instant before dropping into the tunnel.

"You okay?" Jed called.

The flashlight cast a pointless beam against the ceiling. Otherwise it was inky.

"Can you see anything?"

"No. Hand me the flashlight."

The end of the flashlight emerged through the rectangle.

"There should be a turn to the right about fifty feet down," Jed called.

Gregory had to fight the panic that was gripping him. He was no longer certain what was real and what the dream. He feared he would be trapped in the Tombs forever.

After about fifty feet the tunnel turned to the right. Now he was completely on his own. It was pitch dark except for the weird looming shadows from the flashlight. The tunnel smelled of dank water, like an ancient grave. He could feel his pulse beating in his throat.

The small beam from the flashlight reached only a few feet ahead, like the cane of a blind man. He staggered forward. Even the air seemed condensed with the darkness. What if the flashlight went out?

Then suddenly he had reached the end—a concrete wall with a ladder stretching upward. The Emerald Building! He hoisted himself up hand over hand. He wasn't certain whether he would be able to make himself return to the tunnel below.

He lifted the trapdoor at the top. It was still pitch dark. He knew from Virginia that he was in a closet. Power's office was on the other side of the door. The money would be in a corner table in the office. Open the closet door, find the table, take the money, get out of there—it was as simple as that.

Then he fell forward in the dark, banging his shin, and caught himself with his hand, spraining his wrist. The pain brought tears to his eyes. He lay in a stupor, his heart beating wildly. For a moment he must have passed out.

. . .

Gregor was in a stony underground grotto dripping with water. A labyrinth of tunnels stretched ahead, sloping like roots into the earth. For a long time he lay in fear and desolation. Only slowly did he became aware of the other boys, some weeping, others staring into the dark.

Gregor stood up uncertainly, dizzy and nauseated. He tried the oak door. Shut solid. He had to fight despair. Simultaneously, he felt a rising fury—at Principal Alexander, at the professors at the Institute, at his own father. Had they suspected? Had they *known*?

JT sat on a stone ledge at the side of the cave, lost in thought. Gregor approached him unwillingly.

"Now what?" he asked. He could hear the despair in his own voice. He had little trust left in JT. Still, he remembered JT's boast that he was on a secret mission. Remembered the dreamlike conversation with Ariadne (had it really occurred?) in the hotel room. JT still seemed the only hope.

"Get the other guys," JT said grimly. "It's time for a powwow."

Gregor went from boy to boy, rousing them, trying to instill courage. He had to fight the taste of despair in his own mouth.

"Get up, guys—c'mon. We can't just sit here waiting to die. Let's act like Pioneers."

Slowly the boys sat up. Their clothes were damp from the precipitation. Their teeth were chattering.

They gathered around JT, who sat absorbed on his stone ledge.

"The thing with Boob took me completely by surprise," JT said gloomily, as if to himself. "I had no idea they were going to cut his throat."

"What did you think was going to happen?" Lewis asked.

"We've known for a long time that MC has got this thing about bulls. They sacrifice to some kind of creature that lives under White House Square."

The boys sat gloomily digesting this piece of information.

"We've got to find the beast and kill it," JT continued. "That's what I've come for. I was hoping I could do it alone—before we all got trapped down here in this labyrinth. But my mission hasn't changed. We have to seek out the Great Bull and destroy it."

"How are we going to do that?" Fume asked. "With our bare hands?"

"Someone's going to help us—I can't tell you who. But when the time comes she'll help us kill the Great Bull."

"She?" Furst asked.

"Yeah. Stay cool and we'll get out of here alive."

"What about Boob?" Lemon asked.

"I'm sorry about Boob," JT said. "But this is war. You take losses in war. Boob died for the Homecountry. Now it's our mission to finish the job. To see that Boob didn't die in vain. Are we in this together?"

"What choice do we have?" Lewis said. "If we stay here we starve to death—or get our necks cut by that crew back there."

The boys started down one of the tunnels. It twisted and turned into the bowels of the earth. Their clothing stuck to them in the heat. Sometimes they could stand amid flickering eerie light, with puddles of water and cobwebs hanging from the roof; at others it was so narrow that they had to walk single file, bent over, with their hands feeling the sides of the walls. Often they had to keep their heads down or they would bump them.

Sometimes the passages opened into caverns, with puddles of water and stalactites hanging from the rocky roof. In the distance they could hear the cawing sounds of birds. The boys were weak and hungry and bone tired and scared.

"So that's what happens to the Golden Ten," Lewis said to Gregor. "Some honor!"

"This is some kind of a nightmare," Gregor said. "I swear, we must be dreaming. We've just got to find a way to wake up."

"It was no dream," Lewis said bitterly, "when they cut Boob's throat."

Finally the boys came to a stop in a broad open space with a high vaulted ceiling of rock and a small trickle of water that burbled through the center of the cave. Tunnels jutted in all directions. They all drank greedily, then lay down exhausted in various corners.

. . .

. . . lay on the floor of the closet, his heart crashing in his breast. What was he doing? Where was he? How would he ever get out of this nightmare?

Gregory righted himself cautiously. He felt his shin: blood. A great welt. He raised himself, limped forward, found the door to the closet, turned the handle.

The alarm almost knocked him off his feet.

He froze. Time stood still. The wailing screamed about him. Then he leapt forward, scrambling through the room, found the table, found the drawer, swept some bills (he didn't know how many) into his pocket, and, turning (his pants now coated with blood), dove back into the closet, the siren still screeching like some infernal machine that has run amuck.

He landed in a heap at the bottom of the ladder. He was up immediately, groping down the tunnel (was this the right direction?), his eyes straining to recognize some landmark. He had dropped the flashlight.

He ran into the wall.

Then there was silence. In the distance, muffled through many layers, the wailing of the siren.

"Jed—are you there?"

Silence.

"Jed?"

Then, "Yeah—what the hell happened?"

"I dunno. Some alarm. When I opened the closet door."

"Shit!"

Then again silence. Gregory had regained his breath. He was preparing to climb through the opening in the wall.

"Did you get the money?"

"Yeah—I think so. I didn't have much time."

"Well, that's something at least. Climb through. We've gotta get out of here."

Gregory swung up. For a moment he thought he couldn't negotiate the opening because of his wrist. Then his head found the hole and he was pulling himself forward, again aware of his battered shin. He dropped to the ground next to Jed.

When Jed turned on his flashlight, he was holding the gun.

"Jesus, Jed! Put that away."

Jed looked at Gregory. He smiled slowly. Gregory hadn't even known he had the gun with him.

Jed put the gun back in his belt.

"We better not go back the way we came," Jed said. "They might be waiting for us."

Jed dove off down a tunnel. Gregory followed. The thought of being lost in that labyrinth was terrifying, but the thought of Jed and his gun was no better.

The maze turned and twisted; Gregory had no idea where they were. They couldn't hear the siren anymore. They were moving swiftly. Suddenly Jed fell in the semi-darkness, tripping, and Gregory almost piled on top of him.

They lay for a moment, swearing. Jed sat up, and

Gregory could see in the slant beam of the flashlight the dirt on his face. Jed was holding his ankle with both hands.

"You okay?"

"Goddamn it, does it look like I'm okay?"

There was no sound, only their breathing and the distant gurgle of water. Gregory could smell Jed and the stale odor of the earth.

"You sure made a fine mess of it," Jed said, speaking through his teeth.

"How did *I* make a mess of it?"

"Well, I sure didn't set off that alarm."

"Yeah—as if it was my fault. All I did was open the goddamn door."

"Okay, okay. The main thing is to find our way out of this labyrinth."

Then they remained silent, breathing uneasily.

"Let's see the money," Jed said after a bit. "Let's see what we got outa all this."

Jed took the money and started counting it under the flashlight.

"Where's the rest?"

"That's it."

"You only got this? Goddamn it, can't you do anything right?"

"The goddamn siren was blasting in my ears, Jed. We're lucky I got anything."

Gregory was bitterly angry. As if it was his fault the siren had gone off!

"Well, let's get going," Jed said. "There's no use crying over spilt milk. Looks like we'll end up in jail for nothing."

The boys kept limping forward. Gregory's wrist was now hurting badly. Jed's ankle was obviously giving him grief. They proceeded for another twenty minutes, turning and twisting through the dark. Finally Jed stopped and leaned against the wall.

"You know where you're going?" Gregory asked.

"I don't have the slightest idea."

"Great!" Gregory said. "What do you think is happening upstairs?"

"Every cop in this two-bit town must be looking for us."

"Terrific! What'll happen to Virginia?"

"Virginia?" Jed said. "How do I know what'll happen to Virginia? Whattaya got, the hots for Virginia?"

"Go to hell, Jed."

"I think she likes you, y'know that? You can have her if you want."

"You're nuts, Turner. You're really crazy."

"Don't get all snotty, Greg-o. You'd like to have her, so don't act so high and mighty."

It took another forty minutes of blundering before they stumbled onto a ladder. By now they were thirsty and exhausted. Jed had opened his shirt to his navel. All Gregory wanted was to get out of there. He was furious with Jed for the crack about Virginia.

"We'll rest here an hour or so until things quiet

down," Jed said. "Then we'll skedaddle. If we stay around here too long we're gonna land in jail."

Gregory turned his head away. He felt despair creeping over him. How had he ever gotten himself into this maze? How could he ever get himself out? If he could escape from this nightmare, he would return to his mother—Richard or no Richard. He wasn't going to desert her, to chicken out like his dad. The decision had been building in the back of his mind. Jed could keep his portion of the money.

"Where's this girl who's gonna be such a big help?" Furst asked.

"Don't worry yourself about it," JT replied.

All that day the boys had wandered deeper into the labyrinth without finding food, weapons, helper—or the mysterious monster they had to confront. As the afternoon progressed they became more and more tired and discouraged. Finally Fume sat down and refused to move.

"I'm not going any farther," he said. "My feet hurt and I'm tired and I don't feel well."

"What's the point of going any farther?" Babcock agreed. "If there's some bull down here, let it find us. More likely we'll just die of starvation."

"I agree," Luck said. "There's no point in stumbling around anymore. I'm for staying put with Fume."

"If we stay put we'll never get out of here," Lewis said. "They wouldn't have taught us all that self-survival stuff if there wasn't a way out."

"I agree with Lewis," Gregor said. "We have no choice but to push on."

"Get up, Fume," JT commanded irritably. "Enough yapping. Let's get going."

The boys staggered onward through the cave.

"So where's this girl?" Gregor asked JT when no one else was near. He was surprised that Ariadne hadn't showed up already.

JT looked at him and scowled.

"She'll show up—don't worry your head, Levi."

"What if she doesn't?"

"I dunno, genius boy. What do you think?"

"If something doesn't happen soon, we're gonna lose these guys."

JT scowled again.

"Then we'll lose them."

The line began to grow longer as some of the boys straggled behind. Then at some point Fume and Boyer were no longer there.

"I'll go back and look for them," Lewis said.

"Suit yourself," JT said. "I'm pushing on."

Lewis and Gregor held a brief conference.

"I'll try to keep the others together," Lewis said. "If there is some kind of a beast down here, we'll have a better chance if we confront it as a group. You keep up with JT. Keep heading downward. There are fewer tunnels now, they are all converging toward a center."

"Okay," Gregor said. "Good luck." And the two boys embraced quickly.

JT had already departed so Gregor had to run to catch him. He was determined to stay up with JT. He sensed that he was very close to something, some revelation, some understanding.

But he couldn't stay up. He would see JT rushing downward through the caves; then he would be lost from sight; then he would glimpse him again, farther ahead; then he was entirely gone. Passages led downward in all directions, lit by a glimmering light reflected from the walls as from dirty ice. He proceeded with intuitive certainty, as if rushing toward a destination, with growing anguish in his heart. At some time, in some dream, certainly he had been here before.

Occasionally he emerged into larger spaces, caverns glimmering with frost, with the drippings of strange stalactites that depended from the rocky roof like the fangs of beasts. Immense birds roosted in the crags, their wings fanning the air. Bones were piled in corners, the skulls and skeletons of the creatures the birds had fed upon. The birds issued strange cawing sounds that echoed like laughter.

Gregor didn't pause, as if he had lost his balance and had to keep running to stay on his feet. As he proceeded there seemed to be fewer tunnels, he was coming toward the bottom.

"I'll find him," he told himself, though in fact his legs were giving out. His fear and fatigue mixed into a despair that dragged him down. There was a constant murmur of water through the tunnels, and he had to fight the urge to lie down and sleep. He staggered onward, hungry and dismayed, until, overwhelmed, he sank onto a ledge of rock.

After a bit he heard voices. Someone was whispering nearby.

". . . the weapons!" the voice said with great urgency.

"No," she said. "No, I couldn't."

It was JT and Ariadne, but what where they saying?

". . . have to fight him with your hands."

"My hands!"

". . . knows how many he's eaten." Ariadne was explaining something—but what? He lay trying to listen. Everything depended on his hearing! ". . . knows there'll be nine."

"So the others . . ."

"Have to sacrifice them . . . then we'll get away."

Gregor felt stunned. He screwed up all his attention to hear.

"But how will we get out of this labyrinth?"

And then she, "I'll lead you. I've left a trail . . ."

He couldn't hear anymore, they must have moved away. And again Gregor was shaking—but no longer from the cold. They were planning to sacrifice them to this bull! Gregor lay on the ledge of stone overcome by fear, fatigue, despair.

Gregor sat appalled against the wall. The great birds congregated overhead cawing and hooting like men at a prizefight. Bones were piled in corners. For an hour now they had been subjected to the bellowing of the beast from somewhere just next door.

Slowly the other boys had straggled into this antechamber where they huddled, smelling the offal from previous debauches and listening to the ravening howls of whatever it was that awaited them in the farther cavern. They sat looking at each other in dumb amazement, their eyes wide, their jaws chattering.

"What should we do?" Lewis whispered. "What do you think we should do?"

"I dunno," Gregor admitted. "I guess all we can do is face it when it comes."

"But what do you think it *is*?"

"Some bull, I suppose," Gregor said. "Some fucking Minotaur."

He was still stunned by what he had heard JT and Ariadne saying to each other. They were all to be sacrificed to some bull! The Golden Ten! His mind reeled in horror and revolt.

Perhaps if they stayed together they could prevail against the creature, whatever it was. If not, perhaps JT would destroy the thing at the end. At least that would put a finish to this loathsome ritual. At least *someone* would survive.

But how had he gotten into this mess? If he had to die in this stupid, meaningless way, shouldn't there at least be a moment when it all made sense? Or was this all there was, this brutal death at the hands of some stinking creature lost somewhere in the bowels of the earth?

JT stood five feet away looking determined. Ariadne waited by his side. Even now, in what must be the last moments of his life, Gregor saw how lovely she was. How stupid that she should be in love with JT! Was there nothing in life that made sense?

And thinking this, Gregor suddenly felt the instinct to live. The will to survive. If he could, he would prevail. He would escape.

. . . painfully climbing the ladder, Gregory and Jed cautiously emerged. In the distance Gregory could still hear the sounds of police radios crackling. Predawn mist was beginning to rise from the ground. He didn't know where or who he was. Was he still locked in some dream? One thing was certain, he was still up to his ears in trouble.

When he looked back, Jed had drawn the pistol.

"Put that away, Jed. If you don't, I swear, I'm gonna turn us both in."

"If you do, Greg-boy, it'll be the last thing you ever do."

"Are you threatening me?" Gregory said. "Is that what you're saying?"

The two remained staring at each other.

"Just don't turn wimp on me, Levi," Jed said. Then he stuffed the pistol back into his belt.

"We must have gone around in circles," Jed said after a minute. "We're only a few blocks from school. You go and take a look—see what's going on. I'll stay here. But for godsake don't let anyone see you!"

Gregory started down the next block. He wanted to be miles away. He wanted to see Virginia. His mom. He would even settle for Richard. But how could he ever escape from this maze? If he went home he'd just be arrested by the cops.

He paused behind a parked car and could see cop cars beside the school. The red lights from the cars blinked dully in the cafeteria window.

"Well, we've done it all right," he reported when he got back to Jed. "There are cops all over the place."

Jed only scowled. Then he started limping in the opposite direction. He was moving with surprising speed despite his ankle.

"We'll get the bike and get outa here," he grunted. It was obvious he was in pain.

"But—what about Virginia?"

"To hell with Virginia. You interested in the inside of a jail?"

Gregory tried to think but his mind wouldn't work. He had an instinct to walk away. To turn the corner and disappear. But what would he do then?

The motorcycle was parked in a grove of trees on the other side of school. They circled and approached from behind. Jed was limping badly; Gregory's shin had stopped bleeding but ached. He was exhausted. It was almost 6 A.M.

They reached the bike without incident. They could hear the radios from the police cars blaring a block away. They entered the trees where the bike was hidden. Jed wheeled the motorcycle forward, but his ankle gave and he almost dropped the bike. He swore savagely under his breath.

"Hold this goddamn thing, will ya? I'll need to start it with my left foot."

It took a few tries to start the bike. Some chariot of fire, Gregory thought bitterly. The motor roared in the stillness of the dawn.

"They'll hear us."

"Nothing to be done about it, jock-o."

They wheeled the bike onto the street. If anyone saw them now they'd be cooked.

Gregory held onto Jed. He could see how Jed was favoring his foot. Then they were purring down the street. Jed turned the corner and Gregory felt the burst of speed as they leapt forward.

The cop saw them as they turned onto Beacon.

The flashing lights came on immediately; the car headed straight for them. Jed stepped on the motor and they rocketed away. The speed threw Gregory backward; he clutched onto Jed and tried to regain his balance. Jed took the corner fast and Gregory thought he was going to scrape his knee.

"Shit, Jed—slow down."

They were racing toward the edge of town.

Gregory looked back and saw the cop rounding the corner. He couldn't maneuver like Jed. They were gaining ground, but Jed was going too fast.

"You're gonna dump us, Jed."

"Shut up!"

Then he had turned out of town and opened the motor full throttle, and Gregory felt the thrill of it down his spine, the bike banking into the curve. The light of early morning cut the dark. Then they were approaching the bend and the cop wasn't even in sight and Gregory knew they were going too fast and that they couldn't take the curve at that speed and he held on tight as Jed gunned the motor and they flew forward into the darkness and he saw that now and forever they were about to . . .

16

Suddenly the roaring became deafening—the sound froze Gregor's blood. And with that the Minotaur charged into the cavern.

It was a filthy thing, half bull, half man, its hooves striking sparks from the stones, its mouth spewing bloody foam. The great muscle of its hump rippled with unspeakable power. Without a moment's hesitation it charged into Luck, lifted him into the air, and ripped his life out with its teeth.

The boys flew about the cavern in panic. Gregor flattened himself against the wall, his stomach heaving. The immense creature whizzed by and crashed straight into the wall ten feet away. It recoiled instantly and charged again, catching Boyer with one of its horns and dashing him like a rag doll against the stones.

The might of the beast was awesome. It crashed nonstop against the wall. Shaking with fear, Gregor nonetheless watched with care, and he realized that the creature was blind.

Ariadne had raised her veil and was holding it before JT and herself. Instinctively, Gregor slipped along the wall and hunkered down behind them.

Now the beast had chewed Lemon in half.

Blood spattered against the walls. Babcock was crying in a corner. Lifting its head, the Minotaur listened for a moment. Then it charged straight into Babcock, smearing him against the wall like a fly. This charge knocked the ravening beast off its legs. It got up immediately and wandered aimlessly, its dull eyes turning uselessly in their sockets. Then it nuzzled what remained of Babcock, licking the blood.

Gregor could not bear to look at the remains of the four dead boys. The fearsome beast, however, was visibly tiring.

Lewis charged the bull while it was busy with Babcock. He had found a piece of stone, and he clobbered the horrid creature straight between its eyes. With a bellow, with a single toss of its head, the Minotaur flicked Lewis fifty feet across the cavern, where he crashed and splintered against the wall.

So for Furst, for Fume, both of whom were crying

hysterically. Their cries echoed and rebounded about the cavern like rubber balls.

Now the beast wandered drunkenly about the hall, dragging an arm. It paused before the rubbish of each corpse, going back and forth stupidly, as if in senile count.

"Eight little Indians . . . seven little Indians," Gregor repeated to himself in a stupor. "Two little Indians," it suddenly came to him. "Now there are just two little Indian boys!"

"Get him now," Ariadne whispered to JT. And she lowered her veil. The beast rose from its knees and shook its head. It swayed in their direction.

JT glanced backward at Gregor, his eyes crazed with resolution. He reached for him but just then the Minotaur lowered its head and started trotting toward them.

"Get it," Ariadne hissed. "Get it in the eye."

The monster quickened its pace. And in one swoop, JT lifted Ariadne and threw her to the bull.

In that instant Gregor understood JT's plan. The blind Minotaur would cease his ravening after nine victims. Ariadne had been eight. Gregor would be the ninth. JT would escape.

Gregor threw himself against JT, who stood, back turned, still frozen before the horrific spectacle he had created. Caught off guard, JT stumbled forward, and with one twist of his horn the Minotaur caught him in the stomach and tossed him through the air like a sack of potatoes to where he crashed to his death against the bloody stones.

Gregor froze against the cavern wall. If the senile monster couldn't count, he was dead. And indeed the Minotaur stood for a moment uncertain, testing the air with his nose. He was foully ugly, drooling, slathered in blood. He turned his dull head as if to take in the carnage of his mess. Then he sank to his knees. His tail gave a mighty lash. He yawned. He started to feed.

Gregor waited—the longest wait of his life. Finally the Minotaur moved on, farther afield. He was drunk with his feast. Soon he would sleep.

Barely breathing, Gregor inched along the wall. One false move could still rouse this foul fury to action. But no, his haunch turned, the Minotaur was sunk in his own obscene sate.

Gregor sank down in the adjacent cavern. From the distant hall he could hear the echoing snores of the beast.

So that's that, he thought. So that's how it is.

He wasn't sure whether to be glad or heartbroken that he was alive. Lewis was the only hero—Lewis, who lay like a car accident in the farther hall.

Gregor knew that he had to flee, that the Minotaur slept only a hundred feet away; but he slid down exhausted, at the point of utter despair.

He saw a huge man sitting at the head of a table. Suddenly the man fell forward, striking his head, and from his skull there issued a stream of light. Now he was him-self falling downward through the light. At first it was golden, but after a time it changed, rainbowlike, red then blue then purple. As he fell he observed the universe around him, planets and stars and galaxies, tiny and far off, falling like him. When he looked back all he could see was the blackness of space and, sprinkled throughout like tiny points through a lid, the distant stars.

Gregor awoke bathed in longing. He lay staring up into the roof of the cavern, listening to the distant sound of water. And suddenly he remembered something Ariadne had said. That she had left a way out. A thread. The radiant Ariadne, she of the luxuriant hair—was it she who would lead him out after all?

Gregor looked around but he could see nothing. If he could escape he would return home to his mother. Then he observed a silken thread stretching upward into the black. It was barely more than a spider's web. Could something as fragile as that guide him to safety? It seemed unlikely, but what choice did he have? It had to be the trail left by Ariadne, some meager glimmer, even in that darkness, of the future promise of hope.

17

Someone was shaking him. He tried to open his eyes but all was blackness. A thickness of darkness. He had a crashing headache. He could smell the musk of the cave. The dampness. Then he saw a glimmer of light. His eyes adjusted and he recognized that Virginia was shaking him by the shoulder.

"Gregory—Gregory! Wake up!"

"What is it?"

He tried to clear his head. He was still underground, in some cavern.

"Wake up—it's me, Virginia. You've got to wake up."

He sat up slowly, trying to take in what was happening. He couldn't see the roof of the cave, which was lost in shadows, but he could hear the awful sound of the birds flapping their wings and laughing.

"Where am I?"

"Don't you remember—the motorcycle crash?"

Slowly it came back to him.

"Oh, yeah," he said. "What a blast! Where's Jed?"

She turned her face away, and he saw that she was crying. She looked tired, he thought, but still lovely, always lovely, her skin perfect, her hair cut short above her ears.

"He didn't make it, Gregory. He died in the crash."

He sat staring at her. Dead! Jed dead. And again he heard the caw of the birds.

"Jesus! Where am I, anyway?"

But she didn't answer, she only looked away. Then they were silent while he sat thinking, trying to remember it all.

"Gregory," she said after a while, "you've got to try to come back to us. Your mom's brokenhearted. You've got to do it for her, Gregory. You've got to pull through."

The thought of his mother pierced him with pain, but he could smell the smothering emptiness of the cave.

"I'm not sure I can."

"Don't say that!" Again she was weeping. She reached out and clutched his arm. He watched her for a moment, considering.

"Just come back to us," she said.

"Do you want me to?"

"How can you even ask that? You *know* I do, Gregory!"

He saw that she was pleading.

"Okay, okay," he said after a moment. "Don't get so excited." But it was cold underground, and he shivered.

Again they were silent, though tears were running down her face.

"But what's the point?" he said after a pause. "Just tell me that." And he answered his own question. "There is no point."

She was angry now.

"Your question has no point! Are you trying to say there's no point in . . . in what your mother feels for you?"

"No," he admitted. And suddenly the thought of his mother pained him like a blow. "I know she loves me."

"Of course she loves you! And do you think there's no meaning in *that*? What sort of meaning do you think you're looking for?"

But still he shrugged. "Meaning," he said. "Not lots of little meanings. Sure, my mom loves me, but—it's not enough. Not anymore. What about the death of my dad?"

She kept clutching his arm.

"Gregory—do you think your dad's life was without meaning?"

He felt the tears scald his eyes.

"No."

"Do you think he'd want you to die? It would break his heart, Gregory. Don't you know that? It would break all our hearts."

Then they sat, each of them lost in thought, staring at the dim floor of the cave.

"I have to go," she said after a while, scrambling up in the darkness. "I'm not sure I can come back. You're on your own, Gregory. I can't tell you what to do. But, please—come back to us!"

Then she had disappeared into the black, and again he was alone. Tell me that you love me, he thought.

But of course she couldn't. Because it wasn't true. And he heard the cry of the birds. He wanted to sleep. To sleep forever. Narcolepsy, he thought. Jed's fancy word. The love of endless sleep.

But what good would that do? He would just be lost forever in this stupid cave, this labyrinth of dreams. That's what death was, he thought. That wasn't the answer, he saw that clearly now. There was still something else he had to do, but what?

Gregory perceived a trapdoor beneath him. Curious, he opened the door and saw that it lead downward into deeper tunnels. He clambered in and heard the trapdoor swing shut behind him. Then he was descending into the depths of the earth.

He was again in a kind of labyrinth, with passages leading downward in all directions, lit by a glimmering light reflected from the walls as from dirty ice. He proceeded with intuitive certainty, as if rushing toward a destination, with growing anguish in his heart. At some time, in some dream, certainly he had been here before.

Gregory didn't pause, as if he had lost his balance and had to keep running to stay on his feet. As he proceeded there seemed to be fewer tunnels, he was coming toward the bottom. He heard a shrieking bellowing reverberation. Finally he emerged into a level place, a cavern lit with flickering uncertain light. To one side sat the Minotaur, half bull half man, blind, smeared, senile.

The cave smelled bloody, moldy, rotten, foul. Gregory recognized the bones of the other boys lying in heaps, gory and broken. That had been JT. That the beautiful Ariadne, her silken hair still intact. Now the Minotaur had lurched to its feet, was roaming the cavern like some obscene nightmare, some hog or boar that snouted and rooted at the beauty of life. It infuriated him. How could it be that the world should sacrifice to this thing? It seemed to him wholly evil.

Suddenly Gregory was overcome with rage. Advancing, he grasped the Minotaur by the throat. He felt its breath hot on his face, the rank odor from the nostrils like the stench from some slaughterhouse. It was intolerable! He clenched his hands, trying to wring its life—but suddenly he was no longer holding the monster. Suddenly he was holding—his father!

He staggered back. And then the furious words poured from him.

you son of a bitch you coward don't hide down here in the dark

but the man, *I never knew how to awake*

and the boy, *don't give me your shit you're always giving me your shit*

but the man, *i love you*

and then, *i'm afraid dad i'm afraid i'm not sure it's worth it*

but, *we have no choice, son, the worst is in our own heads*

but then, what should i do what should we all do
Listen!
but listen to what i don't hear anything i can't hear
anything i don't know any . . .

Gregory was lying in the dark. He was alone.

And now he saw clearly the other world stretching behind him like a series of rooms through which he had journeyed. Perhaps that was the real world. Perhaps death was just a passing into that world forever. And thinking that, he saw how he loved the light. How he longed to be where he could see things for what they were, not hidden as in a dream. But how would he escape? How would he ever get home?

He made a great effort. It was like rolling a boulder from in front of a tomb. He did not want to be lost forever. He wanted to return home. Far above he could see through the fleecy waters, could hear voices murmuring leaning over eyes peering as from a distance. Then he was surrounded by people—what were they saying? It was time to . . . time to . . .

(but should he turn back to be lost forever in caverns with birds flapping in corners with bones broken and dreams forever dreaming . . .)

NO!!!

And he remembered what his father had said.
Listen!

He was listening *(Do you hear? Do you?)* but at first he could make out nothing. Silence. The sound of blood in his ears. But then, underneath, quiet at first—a rising tide, a ripple, a river. Always present, as the stars are present, though we can't see them in the daylight. *(Can you hear? Can you?)* A beginning. A sustenance. An ocean. A life.

And now he could and now he should and now he would

AWAKE ! ! !